D0952228

Cordially UNInvited

ALSO BY JENNIFER ROY
(coauthored with Julia DeVillers)

Trading Faces

Take Two

Times Squared

Double Feature

Cordially UNInvited

JENNIFER ROY

SIMON & SCHUSTER BOOKS FOR YOUNG READERS

New York London Toronto Sydney New Delhi

CONCORDIA UNIVERSITY LIBRARY
PORTLAND, OR 97211

SIMON & SCHUSTER BOOKS FOR YOUNG READERS
An imprint of Simon & Schuster Children's Publishing Division
1230 Avenue of the Americas, New York, New York 10020

This book is a work of fiction. Any references to historical events, real people, or real locales are used fictitiously. Other names, characters, places, and incidents are products of the author's imagination, and any resemblance to actual events or locales or persons, living or dead, is entirely coincidental.

Copyright © 2012 by Jennifer Roy
All rights reserved, including the right of reproduction in whole or in part in any form.

SIMON & SCHUSTER BOOKS FOR YOUNG READERS is a trademark of Simon & Schuster, Inc.
For information about special discounts for bulk purchases, please contact Simon & Schuster Special Sales at 1-866-506-1949 or business@simonandschuster.com.
The Simon & Schuster Speakers Bureau can bring authors to your live event. For more information or to book an event, contact the Simon & Schuster Speakers Bureau at 1-866-248-3049 or visit our website at www.simonspeakers.com.
Book design by Lucy Ruth Cummins
The text for this book is set in Adobe Garamond Pro.
Manufactured in the United States of America • 0312 FFG
10 9 8 7 6 5 4 3 2 1
Library of Congress Cataloging-in-Publication Data
Roy, Jennifer Rozines, 1967–
Cordially uninvited / Jennifer Roy.
p. cm.
Summary: When eleven-year-old Claire is invited to serve as a junior bridesmaid at the wedding of her cousin, a commoner, to the Prince of England, she learns that another, social-climbing junior bridesmaid is trying to keep the wedding from happening and it is up to Claire to stop her from spoiling the big day.
ISBN 978-1-4424-3920-7 (hardcover)
ISBN 978-1-4424-3922-1 (eBook)
[1. Weddings—Fiction. 2. Bridesmaids—Fiction. 3. Kings, queens, rulers, etc.—Fiction. 4. Social classes—Fiction. 5. Secrets—Fiction. 6. Cousins—Fiction. 7. London (England) —Fiction. 8. England—Fiction.] I. Title.
PZ7.R812185Cor 2012
[Fic]—dc23
2011039052

To Alyssa

Acknowledgments

ROYAL THANKS TO:
The Kingdom of Simon & Schuster Books for Young Readers:
To Lady Alexandra Cooper, for editing excellence and high tea at
the Plaza Hotel; Justin Chanda, Ariel Colletti, and
Amy Rosenbaum; and Lucy Ruth Cummins for her artistry.

THE REALM OF TRIDENT MEDIA GROUP:
To Lady Alyssa Eisner Henkin of Amazing Agenthood
and Lyuba DiFalco

ALSO:
A Burst of Fireworks to Michelle Bisson for helping launch
my career; a Bejeweled Tiara to the Regal Robbin Rybitski;
Cherry Cordial(ly)s to Coleen Paratore; a Noble Steed to
Claudia Aibel; Fairies and Fireflies to the Guarnieri Blaines;
Knighthood to Paul Sheehan; Happily Ever After to
Daphne Chan; and Bows and Curtseys to
Noble Librarians Everywhere

AND SPECIAL GRATITUDE TO MY ROY-AL FAMILY:
Crown Prince Adam of Awesomeness
Countess Julia DeVillers
Queen Mother Robin Rozines
Princess Quinn of Fabulousness
Prince Jack of Jacksland
The Valiant Vermont Roys
And, to King Gregory, for going Above and Beyond

PROLOGUE

The whole world was watching. Waiting. And then, it was time.

The organist began playing the traditional wedding march, and the entry doors opened.

The audience gasped. Framed in the doorway was the most famous bride on earth. She glided in on the arm of her father. Her long, thick auburn hair was up in a loose bun, with small pieces curling out to frame her glowing face. Her bouquet of white irises and pale peach roses was in full bloom. And, of course: The Dress. The dress that everyone would be talking about for weeks afterward.

Wow, I thought. I sneaked a peek at the groom. He was wearing full military uniform, looking polished and handsome. He was grinning. The bride and her father were coming closer, making their way toward the altar. When they reached the front, the bride's father lifted her veil off her face and over her head and kissed her cheek. The bride leaned over to hand her bouquet to her best friend, the maid of honor.

And then the bride looked straight at me . . . and winked!

I gave her a little smile. I was standing perfectly still in the line of bridesmaids, but on the inside? Total jitters. If I hadn't been gripping my own bouquet so hard, I'd have been biting my manicured nails. Thoughts were exploding in my head like fireworks. The evil plot! The love curse!

The moment had come. Would it end up in disaster, with the "I dos" becoming "I don'ts"? Or would goodness prevail, with my lovely, funny cousin marrying her prince and having her dreams come true?

I focused back on the ceremony. The bride and groom were facing each other. It was almost time for the vows! A hush fell over the room.

That's when I opened my mouth. It couldn't be helped—I absolutely had to let it out.

I'm sorry, I thought, tears welling up in my eyes.

And then I did it.

I interrupted the royal wedding of the century.

ROYAL WEDDING COUNTDOWN:
Seven Days to Go

Dear Claire-Bear,

Can you believe it is nearly here? It seems as if I have been waiting forever! The family and fam-to-be are going utterly mad about all the details, but I am trying to stay above the fray. It seems more THEIR wedding, actually. But it will be MY marriage . . . well, OUR marriage, and after all the fuss, THAT will be the reward.

Oh, I'm so glad you will FINALLY get to meet my fiancé and see my lovely city. After all my secret undercover visits to your town, I will finally be able to acknowledge you in public!!!

My secret, darling Cousin Claire, coming all the way across the pond . . . just for little old me! I adore our correspondence—the feel of the pen on stationery, the scented sealing wax. So old-fashioned, but it's also quite fun, don't you think?

Must go—Mummy is shrieking about some nonsense. Love to all! Especially you!

XOXO

B.

"No," I muttered, carefully putting the letter back in the envelope and flopping onto my bed. No, I could not believe there was only one more week until the wedding.

Until a wedding that I couldn't tell anybody about. Not even my BFF Evie, who would absolutely D-I-E.

Not to mention all the kids at school. I would become instantly, miraculously popular. Then I'd have to hang out with Fake Farrah and her Poser Posse.

Hmm . . . maybe it was a good thing it was all hush-hush after all. Because if everybody in this tourist-trap town found out, it'd be the biggest news since the three-eyed frog was found in the lake. (It turned out to be a genetic mutant, not the result of toxic chemicals or anything, so the lake is safe to swim in.)

Anyway.

The news.

That I, Claire Gross (I know, really?) am closely related to Belle—the commoner who is marrying the prince and future king of . . .

"Claire!" my mother called from downstairs. "Dinner!"

"Okay, Mom!" I yelled back, not moving. I stared at a thick ivory card I held in my hands. It was embellished with a gold insignia. The fancy black print said "Cordially Invited." An invitation coveted by millions but granted to only a select few.

And on it in elegant script was my mother's name . . . and mine! My mother was invited to sit among the privileged rows of guests.

I was invited to be in the wedding party.

One would think I would be out-of-my-mind excited to be a royal bridesmaid.

One would be wrong.

BTW, I was a junior bridesmaid. The senior bridesmaids were Belle's friends from University who were like in their twenties.

I'm almost twelve.

But that has nothing to do with why I wasn't excited about the wedding.

It was because I wasn't sure that there's ever a "happily ever after."

"Claire!" my mom called. "Dinner's ready!"

"Coming!" I yelled.

But not quite yet.

I was lying on my bed in front of my laptop. I clicked save and print and shut my computer down.

While my printer spit out pages, I began clearing my stuff off the floor. There were books about the British monarchy—kings and queens, princes and, of course, princesses. I also had a travel guide to London, England, and a folder filled with royal trivia—past and present.

No, I wasn't doing a research paper for history class.

Sput. The last page popped out into the paper tray. I grabbed my latest research and put it in the folder.

This folder held all the information I'd been collecting. It was stuffed full. If Belle truly became a real princess, I wanted to know as much as I could about what her new life would be like.

"Claire Elizabeth!" Mom's voice made me jump a little. "Downstairs, now!"

"Okay!" I called. I put the folder on my desk and headed for dinner.

Walking downstairs, I heard a familiar high-pitched voice.

"It's all so thrilling!" it squealed. "Isn't it, Fred?"

"Umph," another familiar voice grunted.

Fabulous. Fab. U. Lous.

My grandparents were here.

Okay. I love Gram and Grandpa. I'm happy they live only twenty minutes away. But tonight, the dinner table was going to be especially hard to deal with.

I braced myself and went into the kitchen.

"Darling!" Gram exclaimed. "We were just talking about you and the wedding!"

"When aren't you talking about it?" my grandfather muttered, shoveling food into his mouth.

"We brought spaghetti," Gram said. "Now, sit down and tell us everything."

I sat down and immediately bit into a dinner roll.

"Claire's dress arrives tomorrow!" my mom said, as she poured water into our glasses. Except Grandpa's glass. He had already opened a can of soda pop, which I eyed enviously.

"Hello? Earth to Claire!" Mom squealed, as she ladled sauce on top of my angel hair. "Don't you want to tell Gram about your dress?"

"Er, yeah." I focused on twirling my pasta. I'd had three fittings for that dress, and each time was a horror. Imagine being in your underwear and having a strange lady putting a measuring tape around parts of your body that you'd rather not think about. Like my "bust," as the sewing lady had called it. My nonexistent bust that wouldn't keep the dress up. Which is why there were three fittings. They had to "modify" it for my unusual shape.

My cheeks were probably as red as the sauce just thinking about it.

"I just hope everything is all right over there," Gram said.

I stopped chewing. "What do you mean?" My stomach

started to lurch, as I swallowed hard and peered over at Gram, who was fishing for something in the side pocket of her enormous purse.

"I mean this!" Gram said, slapping a magazine down on the table.

"'Will They or Won't They?'" My mother read the headline aloud. "'Prince Caught Kissing Other Girl! Royal Wedding in Chaos!'"

"Guys," I groaned. "That's a tabloid. Just a ridiculous gossip magazine!" I did, however, lean over and peek at the cover photo. Hmm . . . probably Photoshopped. I hoped.

See, over the years that prince fellow had given me reasons to wonder if he was truly THE ONE for Belle.

I knew that my cousin could make her own decisions. I should probably mind my own business. But Belle was THE nicest person I knew, and I had seen her get hurt before. And heartbreak ain't pretty. And when it became global gossip, it was downright humiliating.

Like the time he broke up with Belle, saying he was too young and needed some space. That lasted a whole month!

Or the *second* time he broke up with her, and they told the world they were just on a break. Yeah—a HEARTbreak, for my cousin. I saw the tears.

Okay. Those happened years ago. My mother said that people their age do dumb things. (Like her marrying my father. One more reason that I am skeptical about marriage.)

And to make it all worse—as they always do—the tabloids and gossip blogs came up with embarrassing things to say about Belle and the prince's eight-year relationship: PRINCE TARRIES TO MARRY! SHE'S STILL RINGLESS AND KINGLESS! They nicknamed her NO-WEDDING BELLES.

If the prince really wanted to be with her, wouldn't he put a "ring on it"?

And then . . . he did. And what a ring! A ginormous emerald (her birthstone) surrounded by diamonds.

Belle promised me that I would *adore* (her word) the prince, and that I could trust him to be a loyal and good husband.

"'Prince's Great-Great-Grandmum's Ghost Nixes Nuptials!'" Mom interrupted my thoughts and held up a magazine. "Oh, no!"

"That's bad," Gram said grimly.

Hello? Duh?

"If the prince's ancestors are against the wedding, it would be heartbreaking," Mom wailed. "What could she possibly have against our Belle?"

"Ancestors can be difficult," my Grandmother nodded sagely.

"And so can mothers!" I practically shouted. "And grand-mothers!"

That got their attention.

"Respect your elders," said Grandpa. Then he belched.

Right.

"Sorry," I said. "But over half of marriages fail these days. How do we know the prince is good enough for her? What if he ends up breaking her heart?"

"Oh, Claire-Bear," Gram said. "Everything will be fine. He's a prince!"

"Claire is just being dramatic," Mom said, "when she should just be enjoying herself. Why, a royal marriage is simply so romantic!"

"Not always," I informed them. "Jane, the Nine Days' Queen, thought so until she was executed at the Tower of

London just months after she married Edward the Sixth in 1554. And Anne Boleyn? Beheaded by order of King Henry the Eighth in 1536? Or what about—"

"Pffft . . ." Mom said. "Ancient history."

"And more recent history," I reminded her. "Scandals and divorces and dysfunctional people . . ."

"And deadbeat Hollywood hippies," my grandfather muttered.

"Dad, what on earth are you babbling about?" Mom said. I knew exactly who he meant. My mom—of all people—should be more cynical about weddings.

"Reality," I sighed, spearing a meatball. *Ooh. Spicy.* I reached for my drinking glass.

"Oh, Debra," Gram said. "All children go through phases."

I sputtered, choking a little on the water I was chugging. "I'm just interested in royal families. Historically."

"It was much sweeter when you were into Disney princesses," Mom sighed.

I was a little kid then. What did I know? That was before I'd found out the truth about "happily ever after." I had seen enough Lifetime Channel specials, with my mom sobbing on the couch next to me, to know the reality. The horrible real-life endings.

"It's just that too many marriages start out so good," I sighed. "And then end up so tragic. It's like romance is cursed!"

"Claire-Bear," Mom put a protective hand on my shoulder. "I know you think you know what you're talking about. But there is no curse."

"Because if there were," Gram said. "It would be right here."

She pointed at the tabloids.

"There has been no mention of any romantic curse in *Star*, the *National Enquirer*, or the *Globe*." Gram said. "If it were real, it would be in the news."

"I didn't mean a *literal* curse," I said.

I looked from my mother to my grandmother. Both reddish blonde, both blue-eyed, both in denial. They just didn't get it.

I got my medium brown hair and brown eyes from my father. He'd left when I was a baby to go to Hollywood to "pursue his acting career." Grayson Gross. Of course, eleven years later and no one had ever heard of him. And I rarely heard *from* him. Except when Belle and the prince had gotten serious. Then he'd wanted to use his connections with her to get publicity for himself. But the prince's family would have none of that! They made him sign something that said he'd get in BIG trouble if he contacted a tabloid or blogger or anyone. I overheard Mom tell Grandma that they paid him off. I can't really blame the royal family for silencing my dad. He didn't act like part of their family until something was in it for him. Ugh. My father. All I'd ever really gotten from him was my last name, Gross. What a gift, right? Ha.

"Okay," I said, and changed the subject. "What's for dessert?"

Gram stared at me in horror. "Dessert?" she said. "It's just mere days before the wedding! Sugar can mar a young lady's delicate complexion."

Gram patted my hand.

"Pimples!" Mom said with a gasp. "Claire, she's right. No dessert."

Pout.

"What? No dessert?" My grandfather said, suddenly awake. "We're leaving. And we're stopping at the ice-cream place on the way home."

Dear Claire,

I admit it. I have gotten caught up in all the hoopla. When I first received my engagement ring (which I thankfully still have snug on my finger!), I vowed to focus on the traditional, historical aspects of the event. Britain's past is so rich with its monarchies and fascinating figures. Truly, I want to uphold honor and dignity for our country's future.

But, C-Bear, I can't help it! Everything

looks so beautiful and splendid, I'm now obsessing over floral accents and pastry fillings and the tiny decorative touches on The Dress.

I feel torn. The economy is poor, and our citizens are hurting, so to be so lavish seems inappropriate. But Mummy assures me that the viewers (viewers! I'm marrying before cameras!) want to see beauty and grandeur. That it will be a lovely escape from reality.

Well, it is my reality. Quite daunting, but also quite wonderful. I simply cannot wait for you to join us. You shall be here before you know it!

XOXO

B. (for Bride!)

Bzzzt. Bzzzt. Bzzzt.

My alarm jolted me awake. *Ugh. Monday. School.* I burrowed down with the Beast under my fluffy yellow duvet and contemplated hitting the snooze button. Just a few more minutes . . .

Oh, no. I suddenly remembered.

The kitty litter.

Ugh.

I'd forgotten to do it the night before (and the night before that), and my mother had said I absolutely had to change the Beast's litter box before trash day.

Today was trash day. And the garbage truck came super-early.

I crawled out of bed, leaving the Beast in the cozy nest, and stumbled downstairs.

Yawn.

I tiptoed to the laundry room, dumped the contents of the litter box into a trash bag and quietly sneaked outside.

But first, I looked out the side door. No neighbors. The coast was clear. I ran out in my slippers and made it to the garbage bin without seeing Liam, the high school hottie next door. To be spotted in my ratty old pajamas carrying kitty litter would be the ultimate embarrassment. *Ew. Ew. Ew.*

Not that Liam ever noticed me. But still. I lifted the lid

and dropped the bag with the other garbage. And that's when I heard it.

Click. Click.

What the—?!? I jumped back from the bin of disgustingness and whirled around toward the sound. It was getting lighter, so I could make out a person farther down my street jumping into an SUV with a big red 9 etched on the side.

Too weird.

That clicking. It sounded like a camera! We had plenty of tourists taking photos during the summer season, and in the fall when the leaves changed color. But it was March. Gray, slushy, end-of-winter-not quite-spring off-season. Who would want photos of that?

Then I heard another noise. Liam's family's garage door going up and their car backing out.

Yikes!

I raced into my house, just in time.

Whew. Safety. And warmth.

With a sigh of relief, I turned the water-pressure in the shower to the maximum heat, and proceeded to get ready for school.

An hour later I was schlumping through the halls of school, half-hidden by my hoodie. I tried to convince myself I was embracing my individuality.

"Look!" somebody shouted, as I was walking to homeroom.

"It's *something something* gross," another kid said, his voice partially drowned out by the usual morning locker-slamming chaos.

Yick.

I walked more carefully, scoping the floor for something gross, like vomit or old gum.

I dumped my stuff in my locker and peered into the tiny magnetic mirror. Same boring me. At least I'd had enough time to shower before school after cleaning up the Beast's mess. Now *that* was gross . . .

When I walked into homeroom, everyone who was talking stopped.

My heart began to pulse. *Huh?* Nobody ever paid attention to me.

"Breaking news!" Farrah Harris stood up. When Farrah spoke, everybody listened.

I slipped into my seat. Where was Mrs. Brown?

"Trash Girl has arrived!" Farrah tossed her long shiny hair and smiled her evil smile. Then she walked. Over. To. Me.

"Hi, Claire Gross," she said. "Boy, they really named you right."

"I have no clue what you're talking about," I said quietly.

"I'm talking about this," Farrah shoved her iPhone in my face.

OMG.

There was a photo of me. On her phone.

And . . .

"I look horrible!" I shrieked. Then I clapped my hand over my mouth.

There I was, standing over the garbage can holding a bag of used cat litter, wearing my cruddy old pj's . . .

Click. Click.

I remembered that sound, with the SUV driving away with that red 9 on its side.

The same exact 9 that was on the corner of the picture on Farrah's phone.

News. Channel. Nine.

I was on the news?

"Claire Gross?" A voice came over the loudspeaker, which usually broadcast our morning announcements. "Claire Gross, please report to the principal's office."

"Trash Girl," someone snickered. The whole class started laughing.

Everyone, of course, except me.

3

Dear Belle,

Whenever the kids at school get on my nerves, which is a lot since I got to middle school, I think about how awesome my life really is. And nobody knows it. It's my own happy, magical secret.

Remember when we met the first time at the airport pickup? I was so little, and when I saw your long, dark hair and the book you were carrying, I was like "It's Belle!" b/c you looked exactly like my favorite Disney princess. Who knew that

the nickname would turn out to be such a
perfect fit?

Gotta run!

Claire

I ran down the empty linoleum hallway to the principal's
office, which wasn't exactly a place where I spent a lot of time.

"Claire! What's going on? Why'd they page you?" Evie ran
up beside me, breathless. Evie was a true friend. She'd managed to get a hall pass from her homeroom the second they
paged my name.

"I'm not really sure," I said, blinking back tears. "But somehow my taking out the kitty litter made the top local news."

As we reached Principal Morales's office, we found the
school nurse, a lunch lady, and two secretaries crowded
around one of the ancient computer monitor screens.

"Now for our top story," the anchorwoman announced. "A
local girl's family has been linked to the British royal family and
may also explain the annual disappearance of the princess-to-be."

The screen showed a photo of Belle, with the words ROYAL
MYSTERY FINALLY SOLVED!

And then, it switched to the awful picture of me.

"What?" Evie burst out.

Principal Morales swiveled around in his chair behind the glass door that separated his office from reception to face us. He jumped up and came out to talk to us. But first, he made the secretary shut off her computer.

"Claire," he said, "I've spoken to your mother and she agrees that it would be best for you to go home and deal with this . . . situation."

"Dad!" Evie cried out. "I need to talk to Claire."

"Well," he hesitated. "All right. You can come with us to meet Claire's mom at the front entrance. Be there in five minutes."

He took off in a long stride down the hallway.

"Is it true?" Evie asked. "Do you have something to do with the royal family?"

"Um, yeah," I confessed. "But I was sworn to secrecy."

"Wait." Evie stopped abruptly. Her voice echoed in the empty hallway.

Uh-oh. Evie's face was turning red. I had never seen her look like this. She was usually so mellow and easygoing.

"You lied to me?" said Evie. "You're supposedly my best friend!"

"Evie," I said. "I am truly, truly, truly sorry and I wished

I could tell you so many times. But now I finally can, and I really need my best friend."

No response.

"It's my cousin. Well, really my dad's cousin's daughter or something. Anyway . . ." I kept going. "She needed a place to stay where she could feel normal, so she ended up with Mom and me every summer."

"You don't mean your cousin Belle from Australia?" Evie finally looked at me. "The one I've never met because I've been away at band camp?"

"She's actually from England," I said quickly. "And she's really the future princess and future queen because she's going to marry a prince."

Evie looked at me like I had two heads.

"It's true," I insisted. "Why do you think I'm on the news?"

"Hm . . ." Evie said. "Because of the ginormous secret you've been keeping from me?"

"I *am* sorry," I repeated. "Can you forgive me?"

"Okay," Evie said.

"That's it?" I asked. "I don't have to beg or clean your room or anything?"

"No," she said. "I'm good."

"Evie, you're the best!" I said.

"I know," she agreed. "Now tell me the truth."

"The truth is my cousin's going to be a princess, and I am freaking out," I said. "Because of rumors and royal romances and happily NEVER after. . . ."

"Claire," Evie's eyes widened. "This sounds straight out of a fairy tale!"

I looked straight at her. "Well, believe it or not, it's my real life."

Dear Claire-Bear,

Just call me Snow White, for these days I am trailed by a cadre of protectors. Of course I am not speaking of dwarves but of the security chaps. Who are not diminutive creatures whistling while they work but are beefy bodyguards speaking into their earpieces. Half the time I think they are conversing with me, and I respond. Just call ME Dopey!

Oh, my handsome prince just came in and invited me to dinner and a movie. Hurrah!

It has been a while since we have gone out alone. OK, we won't exactly be alone with the security swarm following our every move!

Well, perhaps I can convince my fiancé to see a chick flick. I can have a chuckle about the mostly-male bodyguards having to sit through it. Wicked, aren't I? ☺

XOXO

Belle

Plantagenet, Lancaster, York, Tudor, Stuart, Hanover . . .

"Claire, you're doing that thing again," Evie said.

"Huh?" I said. "What thing?"

"That thing you do when you're worried," my best friend told me. "Reciting the English kings."

I was doing that out loud? Oops.

Evie and I were in the backseat of the car while my mom drove us back to my house. Evie had convinced her father, aka the principal, that as my BFF, she would have people all over her at school trying to get information and causing a scene. So she also got out of school, and it was decided that she would hang out at my house until her mother could get out of work and come pick her up.

"It's actually a list of the British monarchy houses," I said. "And there are just as many queens. Like today's queen is from the House of Windsor."

"Claire!" Evie gasped and grabbed my arm. "Are you going to actually meet the QUEEN? That's so unbelievably *exciting*!!!"

"Well, yeah," I said. "I've been practicing my curtsy. Knowing me, I'll probably step on her foot or something . . ."

Evie eyed me sympathetically. She knew how klutzy and downright mortifying I could be. Like when I wore my shirt inside-out to school, advertising size large.

And when I tripped on the stage steps at grade school graduation, as I went to accept my perfect attendance award, and sprained my ankle. Causing me to miss the last day of school (officially invalidating my perfect attendance) and be absent for the only *good* school event—the ice cream social.

And the scary haircut of grade 4, the world's loudest hiccups of grade 5, and the red paint spillage incident which made the art room look like a murder scene in grade 6.

Yep. I had a knack for embarrassing myself. It was horrible enough to do it in front of my classmates, but my cousin's wedding was going to be a much, MUCH larger audience.

Ulp.

"We're home, girls!" Mom said cheerily. "Hang on!"

Suddenly our car swerved and zoomed between two news vans, up our driveway, and into the garage, where my mom hit the brakes just in time.

"Whoo-ee!" Mom said. "Still got my stock car racing skills. Take that, paparazzi!"

Evie and I just sat in shock, afraid to take our seat belts off. As the automatic door closed behind us, I could hear people yelling, "Just one shot!" and "Tell us *your* side of the story!"

Bong . . . bong . . . bong . . . bong . . . My mother's cell phone went off. Her ringtone was the bells of Big Ben.

"Hello?" Mom said. Then she turned around and held the phone out to me. "For you," she said.

I took it. "Hello?" I said.

"Claire-Bear!" A very familiar, very British voice crossed over the many miles into my garage.

"Belle!" I gasped. "Omigosh, you wouldn't believe what's going on here! It's insanity! I'm so excited to hear you live in person!!!"

"Let me hear her!" Evie was bouncing up and down so hard the car started shaking.

I switched the phone to speaker. "My mom is here," I said. "And so is my friend Evie."

"Hello, my American mum!" Belle called through the phone. "And Evie, hullo, it is a pleasure to finally speak to Claire's best pal!"

"Aaaah!" shrieked Evie. "She knows who I am! I think I'm going to faint! Aaaah!"

"Evie just found out who you really are," I said, covering her mouth to shush her up. "Sorry."

"No, no," Belle said. "I'm glad this is finally out in the open. I'm just so dreadfully sorry about the trouble it's causing you. And that's the reason for this call."

Oh, no, I thought. *I'm too much trouble. They're not going to want me there after all.* I slumped into my seat.

". . . So if it's quite all right," Belle was saying, "I've asked the staff to arrange a flight and lodging a bit sooner."

I sat back up. "How sooner?" I said.

"She means how *much* sooner," Evie butted in. I elbowed her, and she gave me a little kick.

"Tomorrow," said my cousin. "I will be meeting you at London Heathrow tomorrow evening."

Evie and I stopped fighting.

"I'm going to see you tomorrow?!" I shrieked. Our original plan was to leave Thursday, so this was two whole days earlier! Imagine—just hours ago I was still thinking this was going to be a regular day. But now . . . My mom smiled at me from the front seat and gave me a thumbs-up.

"London, England!" I screamed. "Here I come!"

"The royal wedding!" Evie screamed.

"Pardon? Excuse me?" The little Belle voice came out of the phone. "Is that a yes?"

"YES!" Mom and Evie and I said. Then I felt a little embarrassed, because we *were* speaking to the fiancée of the prince of England.

"I mean, that would be delightful," I said in a more mature, proper tone.

"Hurray!" Belle yelled. "Woo-hoo! That rocks!"

Oh, yeah. She may be the world's newest princess bride, but she's still *my* cousin.

"YOU rock!" I yelled back, giggling.

"You rock *more*!" Belle shouted.

And as we ended the call, we were all laughing.

Dear Belle,

Usually, I would write this letter, stick an airmail stamp on it, write your special anonymous post-office-box address on the envelope, and put it in my mailbox. This time? I will be handing it to you in person! Woo-hoo!

Right now, I'm kicking back in my FIRST CLASS airplane seat on my way to London Heathrow Airport. I. Cannot. Believe. It. I have my own personal TV, and the flight attendant brought me a special dessert—an ice cream sundae topped with crumbled shortbread cookies. Very British. Very delish.

The only other time I've been on a plane was a trip to Pittsburgh to visit my grandma's old friend. They served packets of dry pretzels. Being Claire-the-Royal-Cousin is a million times better than being plain Claire Gross. Everything would be perfect if only Mom would stop snoring.

Last night, Evie helped me pack. I told her how you were starting to become more famous at the same time Hannah Montana came on TV, so I came up with the idea that you should wear a disguise. When I showed Evie pictures of you from my secret scrapbook, she laughed so hard. I mean, you look TOTALLY different in that funky blond wig with the pink stripe and your fake nose ring. I personally think you rocked the look, but I suppose it wouldn't go over so well in the royal palace. Hee.

OMG, the pilot just announced our desent decsent heading down to land. AAAAAH! So

excited—SEE YOU SOON!
   Love,
   Claire

I grabbed my travel bag and unzipped it. I took out my lip gloss and a breath mint. As I stuffed the bag back under the seat in front of me, I checked out my new red Wellies. The boots had arrived at my house just in time in a special delivery package from Belle! Also in the package were two London travel passes, a credit card for my mom and . . . a cell phone for me. MY! FIRST! CELL! PHONE! It had a touch pad and video screen, so I could Skype Evie.

That was important. Because I was counting on Evie to help me check out this prince guy who wanted to marry my cousin. Sure, I'd read all about him and heard lots of stories. But meeting someone in person was different. I needed to see for myself that Belle would be okay.

The plane landed. Touchdown England! My mom woke up, and we were the first ones off the plane and into the airport. Our instructions were to go straight through customs.

"There's the 'Customs' sign, Mom." I pointed. There was a

crowd of people. Yikes, this might take forever.

"Debra and Claire Gross?" A man with an official-looking uniform approached us. "Come with me. I shall take you to Customs."

I looked at my mom, who shrugged. We followed the man, who held up a badge. The crowd parted and let us walk all the way to the front, where a door that said CUSTOMS OFFICE opened. Mom and I were swooped inside. And then the door behind us closed.

Inside the room were security people. And one woman in a huge, floppy hat, dark sunglasses, and a long trench coat.

"Belle!" I shrieked, and ran to hug her. No disguise could fool me.

"Claire!" Belle tucked the shades in her pocket and then hugged me back. Hard. "You're here! And Aunt Debra, I hope your trip was not too taxing?"

My mom came over and kiss-kissed Belle the European way, on both cheeks. I let go of my cousin and stepped back. Belle smiled her glow-white smile and told the security people we would be leaving the airport.

"It has been an honor to serve you, milady," said the officer who had first greeted us.

Belle put her sunglasses back on and kept her head down. We made our way through the airport completely surrounded by security people. We moved as if we were a single organism, with mom, Belle, and me as the nucleus. Finally, we reached the exit, where a l-o-o-o-ng black limousine was waiting. For us!

"I can't believe you actually came to the airport!" I said to Belle, as we sat in the back of the limo.

"It was very thoughtful of you," my mom added.

"Well, I did not want your first impression of London to be a bunch of stern-faced guards in uniform!" Belle said. "You're family! Of course I'd be here."

"May I Skype Evie?" I asked my mom. She looked at Belle.

"Please do," Belle said. "I'm sure she will be pleased that you've arrived safe and sound."

Well, that too. I really wanted to show Evie the inside of this limo. TV! Soda bar! Light dimmers! A minifridge with chocolates—even better tasting than American chocolate! (I had already eaten a Cadbury Crunchie and a Galaxy bar. Yum times one hundred.) I video chatted Evie. When her face came on the screen, we both screamed. Mom rolled her eyes.

"Sorry," I said meekly to Belle.

"Allow me to say hello," Belle said. She'd taken off her sunglasses and hat and looked amazing.

"Hi, Evie!" Belle waved into my cell.

"Hi, Your Royal Majesty Highness—I don't know what to call you. Should I curtsy or bow? Claire! Help!"

I turned the phone around so Evie could see me.

"She's not married yet," I informed her. "She's still just Belle."

"Oh, right," Evie said. "Sorry."

"It's okay! Let me take you on a tour of our fancy limousine," I said. "Here we have the soda pop bar, and here are the plush leather seats." I stopped. "Belle, can she see through the window? I mean, I could show her the streets going by."

"Doubtful," Belle said. "The windows are made of special bulletproof glass and are quite thick."

Gulp.

That's when I realized how serious this all was. There have been terrible things like assassinations all throughout history.

"Claire-Bear," Belle said. She leaned over the seat and tucked a piece of my hair behind one ear. She used to do the same thing when she visited, and for some reason it always made me relax. I took a deep breath and let it out.

"Now, let's take a look into the fab-u-lous minifridge!" I said, in my best game show host voice. I opened the fridge door and held the cell phone inside.

"Cool!" Evie's voice came out of the fridge. "Chocolate! And little bottles of water! And . . . what's in the container?"

"Oh, that," Belle laughed. "That's my leftovers from dinner—a chopped liver sandwich on sourdough bread. A bit of a treat on my otherwise strict prewedding diet."

Silence. I knew Evie and I were thinking the same thing. Chopped liver—a treat? Ew.

"Well." My mother finally spoke up. "I simply cannot wait to hear all about the wedding plans, down to every single detail."

"M-o-m," I groaned. So embarrassing.

"I look forward to that, Aunt Debra," my cousin said brightly. "But look! Here we are at your hotel!"

"Gotta go, Evie!" I shut down Skype and started to climb out of the limo.

"Wait, Claire!" Belle said. "Just your mum is going in for now. There's the bellhop, ready to take all the luggage, Debra."

I looked out the open door my mom had just climbed out of. Yep, there was another man in uniform.

"At your service, ma'am," he said, piling our suitcases on a cart. My mother giggled. Yeesh.

"I'll see you later tonight!" Mom called to me. "Have fun and mind your manners . . ."

The limo started pulling away, leaving Mom behind.

I looked at Belle. "What's going on?" I asked. "Where are we going?"

Belle laughed. "Surprise!" she said. "There is a dinner tonight at Buckingham Palace! I thought it would be a nice way to introduce you to some of the people who will be in the wedding. Most importantly, you can meet my darling fiancé!"

"Dinner," I said. "Tonight. Palace." I swallowed hard. Royal people judging me? "Trash Girl" Gross from Lake George, New York? And speaking of *gross* . . .

"I'm a mess!" I shrieked. "I have travel stink and seat hair! And I'm wearing jeans! I can't go, Belle! I'm hideous, and I have nothing to wear!"

"Stay calm, Cinderella," Belle said. "Do you really think I wouldn't take care of you? When we arrive at the palace, I'll take you in the back service entrance and bring you up to a suite. No one will see you, I promise."

"And then?" I asked.

"Then you will bathe and put on a robe. Your stylist will be there to help you choose your clothing and do your hair."

"My *stylist*?" Ooh, Evie would be so jealous!

"Actually, she is one of my dear friends from University," Belle said. "Margaret is a genius stylist. Without her, I would have been unmercifully slain in the press. So first, she'll get you ready. Then, dinner. And afterward, the limo will take you to the hotel to meet your mum and get some sleep. Sound all right to you, Claire-Bear?"

I was speechless.

I nodded my head yes.

I might never be a real princess, but it looked like I was about to have the royal treatment.

The limousine stopped. The chauffeur came out and opened the door. Wowza. We were at Buckingham Palace.

ROYAL WEDDING COUNTDOWN: *Four Days*
ROYAL DINNER COUNTDOWN: *One Hour*

```
EV—I'm going to The Palace! To
meet my stylist!! To get ready
for a dinner with the Royals!!
Eeeeeeee!!! This is surreal!
Wish u were w/me! C
```

We made our way through hallways and rooms on our way to my "dressing room." Belle walked so quickly, I didn't have time to appreciate all the beautiful paintings and sculptures and chandeliers. Not that I would have known anything about them.

We also passed a few people, who said "hullo" with a smile. Nobody famous. Moving on.

"Come in here, Claire." Belle opened the door to a small-ish room. Then she squealed, "Mags-Bags!"

She ran over to the only person in the room, whose head was buried in a hanging rack of clothes. There were shoes all over the floor, and a vanity table with makeup and hair stuff.

Cool.

The girl pulled herself out of the outfits and pulled Belle into a big hug.

"Beauty!" she exclaimed. "This is it! I told you when we were assigned to be roommates for first year that you would become someone special! I'm a little psychic that way." The girl let go of Belle and looked me over.

"Erm, I just got off the plane, and, I'm sorry," I babbled, "but you don't have much to work with." I looked down, embarrassed to admit my insecurity.

"Chin up, love!" Mags-Bags said. "You just need a little spit and polish and you'll feel like a princess." She laughed.

I looked at her and smiled. A little. She was just so peppy it was contagious. With her cropped, platinum pixie-cut hair and her butterfly tattoo on her ankle, she didn't look like she'd fit in with the royal crowd either. It made me feel better—that maybe they would be accepting of an American tabloid cousin after all.

"Claire, I must be going," Belle said, gliding over and kissing me on both cheeks. "I leave you in good hands. Margaret will take good care of you."

"Oh, is it Margaret now?" Belle's friend said. "At University, Mags-Bags was good enough." She sniffed dramatically.

Belle rolled her big brown eyes and then winked at me. "We called her Mags-Bags at school because she made her own purses and backpacks. Everyone coveted them. I still have the one she created for me," Belle said.

"Yes, well, don't take it out in public," Margaret warned. "Black-studded leather with pink skulls does not mesh with your current wardrobe."

We all laughed.

"I admit I enjoy my new 'royally acceptable' couture," Belle said. "But I am holding on to that bag. I haven't changed completely."

"Not on the inside," I said loyally. Belle blew me kisses and left the room.

"Okay, Claire-Bear," Margaret said. "Let's do it!"

"How did you know Belle calls me Claire-Bear?" I asked. Not *too* embarrassing.

"Tosh, we all have nicknames," my stylist said. "At school there was Paul the Tall, Scott Spots—he had terrible acne, but it cleared up with treatment so he wasn't offended—let's see, Holly 'Wood' Watson, the drama queen . . ."

"And my cousin was Beauty?" I said.

"Yes. Simple and succinct," Margaret said. "I remember back when we were 'introduced' before University by mail. I received a note stating that my roommate would be a Miss Worthington. But once we got to campus, the whole formal names thing was tossed in like three minutes. Now, let's sit you down in this chair, and we'll start with your hair."

I sat down in the swivel chair, which must have been the only non-antique in the palace. As I felt my hair squirted and combed and detangled, I began to relax a little.

"It's funny, because I always thought that Belle looked like the Disney princess from *Beauty and the Beast*," I admitted.

"So if your cousin is Beauty," Margaret said, doing something tickly with my hair, "then the prince is the beast?"

"Uh—no—" I stammered. "Actually, my cat is named the

Beast. He's huge and, well, rather homely. I don't know if the prince is beastly or not. I haven't met him yet so I don't have an informed personal opinion."

"Smart girl," Margaret said. She was now fluffing powder on my face with a poufy brush. "Close your eyes."

I shut my eyes and let her apply makeup, "just some touches," she said, because of my "naturally youthful loveliness." I agreed with the "naturally youthful"—but "lovely"? I thought not.

Swish. Swipe. I was finally beginning to feel comfortable in Buckingham Palace, when . . .

Bang!

The door flew open, and so did my eyes. A little, elderly woman strode into the room after slamming the door open.

"What is this?" she demanded.

"Hello," Margaret said, seemingly not rattled by the intrusion. "Belle told me that this room was available, and that we could use it."

The woman glared at us with beady dark eyes. "Well, I did not authorize it," the lady said, and tapped her foot impatiently.

"There is no need for foolishness on a child of this age. Finish up and tidy up."

She quickly turned around and clomped out the door on her chunky-heeled lace-up shoes. Then she slammed—really, slammed—the door shut.

I hadn't moved or said a word the whole time. Margaret went back to penciling my eyelids.

"Margaret?" I said. "Who was that?"

"Call me Mags," Margaret responded. "Or I'll think I'm in trouble with my mum. And that was Miss Cornelia. Who cannot be escaped, as she has been secretary to the royal family for as long as anyone can remember."

"She's pretty scary," I said. "Belle has never mentioned her to me."

"Oh, your cousin was just trying to protect you," Mags said. "Miss Cornelia is just a bossy cow. No worries, Claire. *Hakuna matata.*"

I giggled.

"I'm sensing a Disney theme here," I said. "Beauty, the hopefully-not-a-beast prince . . ."

"The evil witch, who just made her appearance," Mags

continued. "And then, of course, there's Cinderella."

"Who's Cinderella?" I managed to ask, as gloss was brushed on my lips.

Mags turned me around on the swivel chair so that I faced the vanity mirror.

Whoa.

"You are," said Mags. "Now, we'll just get you dressed and you'll be ready to meet Prince Charming."

"Not my Prince Charming," I corrected, blushing a little. Boy, I wished I could look like this every day. "My cousin's Prince Charming."

"True, you will meet the prince," Mags agreed. "And I do believe you will find him a solid bloke as well as a charming one. But you never know—magical things can happen in a palace, and you might be surprised."

"I'm surprised, all right." I looked at Mags shyly. There was sparkle in her kohl-rimmed eyes. "You just did magic on me. I look . . . nice."

"Nice?" Mags repeated. "Darling, you look more than nice! Look at your gorgeous thick hair and your divine eyelashes! Just like your cousin Beauty's! It's obvious you two are related."

Huh?

I peeked at myself in the mirror and touched my hair, gently, so as not to ruin Mags's work.

Oh. My. Gosh. Could she be right? I had always just tossed my hair back in a ponytail. And focused on my too-big-for-my-face nose. Which, after the makeover, didn't look so big anymore.

I did resemble my cousin! At least from the neck up.

"I've got the perfect dress," Mags announced. "And with these shoes, you'll be comfortable and dazzling, from head to toe. So, when you are presented to the receiving line—"

"The *what* line?" I asked. What had I gotten myself into?

"How about I give you the step-by-step instructions while you put on your new clothes."

"Thank you," I said gratefully. "I need all the help I can get."

Mags flung a large piece of fabric over the dress rack. Instant dressing room. As I was about to go behind it and change my clothes, I had a thought.

"Excuse me," I said. "But how do you know all this ceremonial stuff if you're a stylist? Not that there's anything wrong with styling. I think what you do is amazing, but how come you're so relaxed? I mean, this is Buckingham Palace!"

I wanted to know her secret. She had more poise in her pinky finger than I could ever hope for in my entire *self*.

There was a knock on the door. A person in a white uniform peeked her head in.

"Pardon, Lady Margaret?" she said meekly. "The prince's stepmother has requested your presence for a quick touch-up."

"Tell her I'll be there in a jif," the stylist said.

"Of course, milady." The person bowed her head and backed out.

I looked at Mags-Bags and raised my eyebrows.

"Lady Margaret?" I said. "Lady???"

"Pfft . . . titles." She waved her hand, as if blowing it off. "One is just born into it. But finding your unique style and owning it? Now, that is priceless!"

I checked my cell phone for messages. Nothing. I wasn't sure of the protocol regarding texting in Buckingham Palace, and I saw that I only had one bar, so I shut the cell's power off.

"Miss, it is your turn next," a butler-type person said to me. Oh boy. I'd been practicing for this moment for months. I slipped the phone into the pocket of my new cashmere cardigan. That's right, cashmere—the fabric of the fancy folk. I also wore a new dress, which was strappy with lavender flowers on it, and new silvery, soft ballet shoes.

Belle's friend Margaret had twisted my hair into a kind of tousled bun, an updo I'd only seen on celebrities. And I'd even been given small silver earrings shaped like flowers.

I felt almost pretty. And also pretty nervous. Mags-Bags had prepped me for what was going to happen next, and for what I was supposed to do. But learning stuff and then actually doing it? Not always so easy for me. I thought about all the things that could go wrong. Like saying something stupid, or tripping and falling . . .

"Your turn, miss," the butler said.

I was in the reception area, where the receiving line was. All the VIRs (Very Important Royals) were standing in line, meeting their guests one by one.

I suddenly felt very alone. At home, I was now known as Claire-the-Trash-Tween. Here? I wasn't known at all. Claire-the-Who-Cares? That was me.

"Presenting Miss Claire Elizabeth Gross!" a uniformed man called out loudly.

Here goes nothing. Or Nobody, I should say. I walked forward on shaking legs and stopped to face the first person in the receiving line. It was a long line. If I fell now, I'd knock the whole line of people down like dominoes.

I managed to stay upright and said hello to the first person. It was the queen's husband. (Not called a king, BTW. His actual title is Prince but, to avoid confusion, Belle just calls him the queen's husband.) He held out his hand and I placed mine in it. Then he kissed my hand and said, "Welcome, young lady."

I took my hand back awkwardly, gave a little head bow and said 'Thank you, sir.'"

And next in line was . . .

The queen! *The queen!* The queen of England!

I thought back to famous British monarchs before her. Like Queen Victoria, who ruled at the height of the British Empire, when Britain controlled one-fourth of the world's land and people. And Queen Elizabeth I, who ruled during Shakespeare's time and whose powerful personality was legendary. And now I was face-to-face with a Real Live Queen!

She stood very straight and regal. She wasn't very tall, maybe just an inch taller than me! She was wearing a cream-colored suit and would have looked like a typical gray-haired grandmother except for the humongous necklace of jewels around her neck. Rubies, sapphires, diamonds . . . the most dazzling jewelry I'd ever seen. Oh yeah. This was true royalty!

And the way she looked at me? Serious. No hint of a smile or any warmth.

Gulp.

I curtsied down low, as I'd been taught, saying, "Your Majesty." I straightened up, and saw that the queen had moved on to the next person behind me.

Was that it? Did I just get dissed by the queen? Or was it normal to move on so quickly?

I had no time to think about it, because I had to make my way down the line. The prince's father smiled at me after I bowed my head, making me feel a little better. His wife, the prince's stepmother, also smiled. (The prince's own mother had died in a royal tragedy before I was born. My mom said it was a really sad time.)

Next there were the prince's aunt and uncles to bow to. And Belle's parents, who each gave me a hug and said how wonderful it was to finally meet me. And a political guy whose face I sort of remembered from social studies class. And his wife. I nodded and smiled. By this point I was feeling like a bobblehead.

Finally! I'd reached the last two people in line. The two most important people.

"Belle," I said, curtsying—even though I didn't have to. Belle wasn't officially royal yet.

"Claire." Belle smiled. "You look lovely. Now let me introduce you to my fiancé."

"Hullo," said the prince. The. Prince. Live in person. I did a shaky curtsy. Mags had told me I was supposed to address him by his title, but he was taller and handsomer than I'd expected. He was wearing a formal black tuxedo, with a gray vest buttoned over a lighter gray shirt, with a gray silk tie. In his jacket pocket a red handkerchief stuck out, and an assortment of official-looking badges, medals, and ribbons adorned his lapel.

I'd read all about the prince's military honors, his royal titles, his impressive uniforms. But seeing him, in person, in a fancy tuxedo, I could see why he'd been named "The World's #1 Catch." *Whoa.* All words flew out of my head.

"Yerp," I said.

Belle giggled.

"He has that effect on all the women," she said, nudging her fiancé. "You would not believe how many girls—and grown women—have to be revived after fainting."

The prince cleared his throat. "Yes, quite embarrassing actually," he said. "On hot days they just drop like flies." Then he winked at me. The prince winked! "Claire, I look forward to spending a bit of time with Belle's 'awesome' American cousin later," the prince said, and grinned. He had a lot of shiny teeth.

"Er," I stammered. "Yes. Thank you. Cheerio."

Cheerio? Who am I, Mary Poppins?

Just then a woman in uniform took my arm and led me away from the line.

Well, that went well, I thought, blushing. Okay, how was I supposed to evaluate the prince if I couldn't even speak intelligibly when he was around?

I still felt a little dazed, so I was relieved when Uniform Lady guided me down to the far end of a l-o-o-o-ng table where there were empty seats, and pulled out a chair. It was definitely an antique chair. I wondered what other famous and infamous people had sat on it. Maybe I could ask Uniform Lady; I didn't want her to think I was too snooty to talk to the help. She would probably love to share a story or two.

"Mademoiselle," she said, pushing my shoulder down so I'd sit. I sat. And then she disappeared.

There were many people already seated at the table, but I

felt completely alone. And stupid. What to do now? I picked up the place card that had my name written in calligraphy. How did they get the *C* so swirly? This was definitely going to be a souvenir.

And the napkins? Deep burgundy cloth fashioned into ducks—no, swans. I lifted a small spoon. Shiny silver. Also ancient-looking. I wondered who else had eaten from this very spoon. I'd be wondering a long time, I guessed, since no one was around that I could talk to.

And then a girl sat down to my left.

She looked about my age, but way more sophisticated. Her glossy black hair hung sleekly down her back; she wore a black strappy dress and—yikes—high-heeled sandals. Very high heels.

I checked out her placecard. Pandora. Her name was Pandora? Wasn't that the name of someone in a Greek myth who unleashed horror on the world?

"Are you a junior bridesmaid, too?" I asked her, determined to be friendly.

"Yes," she responded without looking at me.

"I'm Claire," I said, giving it one more try. "I'm Belle's

cousin from America, and I've never been out of the country before today—"

Pandora interrupted my babbling. "You don't say."

I shut up. I could take a hint. I picked up a heavy crystal glass and sipped at my water. Oops. My sip was more of a slurp.

Pandora sighed loudly.

What? I double-checked. Yep, it was my water glass, not hers. For the last three months, ever since I had known I was going to be in the wedding, I had been watching online videos teaching proper dining etiquette. I'd learned manners for a fancy dinner, which had included memorizing fancy place settings, so that I'd know which utensils to use and stuff.

"I've been paired with a child," Pandora grumbled, glaring at me.

"Pandora, play nice," someone said from across the table. I looked over and saw a boy sitting down in a chair.

A very cute boy.

"Oh shut it, Symonds," Pandora frowned.

"I'm Tristan Symonds," the boy said to me. "And this bloke here is Callum Duff, boy genius."

Another boy had cruised up to the table in a motorized wheelchair.

"Greetings," the boy squeaked. He had white-blond hair that made him look a little like a Q-tip.

"Duff, Pandora, and I have all been in school together since nursery," Tristan said.

"Boffins," Pandora said, rolling her icy green eyes.

"Boffins are in," Callum Duff said, "Hot, trendy, and ready to rule the world."

I was completely lost.

"Um," I said. "What's a boffin?"

"A nerd," Tristan said matter-of-factly. "Also referred to as geeks. Duff and I, besides being boffins, are junior grooms-men for this lovely occasion. And yourself?"

I decided I liked this Tristan guy. Not to mention that he was as good-looking as a TV actor, with brown wavy hair and intense blue eyes.

"I'm Claire. I'm eleven and a half years old, and I'm Belle's cousin," I responded. "I live in New York."

"New York City?" Pandora perked up and turned to look at me.

"No, Lake George," I said. "It's this vacation town about three hours north—"

"Never mind then." Pandora shut me down. Oh. Kay.

Uniformed staff began bringing out small plates of food. Mine had some little mini-appetizers. I tried a mushroom-stuffed pastry. And a shrimp dipped in cocktail sauce. Then I popped a cheese biscuit into my mouth. Yum. All very yum.

"Charming," Pandora said. "Now I'll have to deal with your garlic breath all evening." I noticed she had only eaten one appetizer—a baby carrot.

The cheese biscuit *had* been very garlicky. I drank more water, hoping to dilute my possible garlic breath.

"So, Claire," Pandora was saying. "As head junior brides-maid, I am responsible for keeping up the standards at all times. I will need to evaluate your walk down the aisle—your pace, carriage, and placement of hands for the bouquet!"

What?

"Did you just say you're head junior bridesmaid?" I asked. No one had mentioned it to me.

The staff swooped in and exchanged our plates—angel hair pasta in cream sauce.

"Of course," Pandora sniffed. "I *am* a certified royal wedding expert."

I glanced over at the boys, to see if they knew what she was talking about, but they were both chowing down pasta.

"I attended the prestigious Princess Prep Programme," Pandora continued. "Two weeks in Kensington of intensive training in advanced etiquette, diplomatic skills, fashion, and gala hosting."

Suddenly my table setting memorization and curtsy preparation seemed rather weak.

The boy named Callum looked up from his food.

"Congratulations," he said. "Did you have a graduation party with a crown-shaped cake and pink balloons?"

"So," Pandora ignored him, "I shall have my social secretary contact yours, Clara, and we can set up an instruction session. Don't worry, I'll make sure you don't embarrass yourself during the wedding festivities."

Um, thanks?

I wasn't sure what to say. On the one hand, Belle hadn't mentioned anything about a head junior bridesmaid. On the other hand, I certainly wasn't confident about being around royalty. I could use all the advice I could get!

"Maybe you could give me one tip right now," I suggested. "What's one thing I should do?"

"Hmmm . . ." Pandora thought for a moment. "I recommend you try not to say anything. With your accent, it's obvious you are a Yank from the sticks."

What?

She *did not* just say that. That was so mean! But what could I do? I did not want to make a scene. I kept quiet.

"Your entrée, miss." A wait staff guy took away my untouched pasta and slid a larger plate in front of me in one fluid motion.

I concentrated on the next course. I took a bite of glazed ham. Then a bite of mashed potato. Then a sip of water.

"The most important thing we'll need to work on is your appearance," Pandora said in a low voice. "I, of course, will be photographed and filmed quite a lot, and when the cameras are on me, I don't want the shot ruined. So, I will show you how to stand and what facial expression to use and, basically, how to not embarrass the position of junior bridesmaid."

I froze. Okay. That *was* my secret fear. What if I embarrassed the royal family?

What if I let Belle down?

Wait. . . . What if I came all the way to England to be bullied by the British version of Fake Farrah???

8

(Letter dated two months before . . .)

Dear Belle,

I'm sorry, but I can't be in your wedding. I'm
scared I might mess things up . . .

(. . . crumpled paper found on bedroom floor by the Beast,
who batted it around the house for an hour before I threw it
in the garbage.)

I carefully ate a few more bites of my meat and potato. I
glanced at Pandora, who was nibbling on an asparagus. She
looked smug.

And that's when it hit me. Back home, I was insecure,

invisible Claire Gross. Let's face it—I was a total boffin.

But here? I was Belle's cousin. The bride's favorite cousin.

"You know," I said. "You, Pandora, may be studying to be a princess, but obviously the prince thinks my cousin is already perfect princess material. And she says I am her perfect choice for junior bridesmaid.

"So I don't need your advice or your approval, thank you very much."

I heard Callum laugh. Encouraged, I looked up to see Tristan crack a smile. Oh yeah. Take that, Mean Girl.

"You have no idea about anything," Pandora hissed, quieter now. "I am a Brit! My family has been VERY closely linked to the royal family for centuries. You, American Girl, are here simply because you are distantly related to a commoner who believes she should marry the prince."

"What do you mean, 'believes she should marry the prince'?" I said. "She is marrying the prince. So there. Ha."

"Really, Pandora," Tristan spoke up. "You're being quite rude. Is that how they taught you to behave in Princess Prep?"

"And another question," Callum said, pointing his fork at Pandora. "What exactly were they 'prepping' all those girls for? It's not as if there are hordes of princes to go around."

"You two know nothing," Pandora spat. "Becoming a princess is my destiny."

"Fantasy," countered Callum.

"Reality," stated Pandora, glaring at the boys.

"Well, anyway," I broke in, not really sure where Pandora was going with this, "marrying this prince is my cousin's destiny. And she's going to be the most beautiful princess bride ever."

And then I felt a sharp, spiky heel come down on my foot.

"Ow!" I whimpered, jumping up a little from my seat. *Don't make a scene,* I told myself. I was trying to sit back down gracefully, when . . .

"OW!!!!" I yelled, jumping back up from the chair, which fell backward onto the floor with a huge *CRASH.*

I had sat down on something sharp. And painful. I looked down and saw my cocktail fork on the floor by the chair. I'd sat on my cocktail fork. Then I looked up.

The entire royal dinner party was staring at me silently, as I stood holding my sore rear in my hands.

I felt tears well up in my eyes. I looked around for the nearest exit. I had to run and hide and never come out and . . .

"Hear, hear!" a male voice boomed from the head of the table. It was the prince! "Now seems the perfect moment to introduce you all to a very special person, my fiancée's cousin Claire, who's come all the way across the pond to help us celebrate."

I dropped my hands, still standing. A waitperson had quietly picked up my chair behind me. The prince was looking at me and smiling his toothy grin. He continued his speech.

"Claire is just one of the many reasons why I am so delighted to be joining Belle's family. So, let us raise our glasses and give a warm, royal welcome to Cousin Claire."

"To Cousin Claire!" people said, lifting their glasses and clinking one another's.

"Pandora?" Callum Duff leaned forward, glass held up. "You are not 'cheersing.'"

"Urghh!" Pandora folded her arms and made a rather unprincessy noise. "'Cheersing' isn't even a word."

"I'll 'cheers' to Cousin Claire," Tristan said. He clinked his glass against Callum's, his blue eyes looking at me as he sipped from the glass.

Oh. That boy was seriously adorable. Just looking at him made me feel a little better. Still foolish, but better.

Then, things got a WHOLE lot better.

"Claire!" Belle called out. "Come sit with us up here for sweets!"

"Yes, please do," agreed the prince. He said something to a waiter, who found an extra chair and placed it between the happy couple.

I got up from my seat, and I carefully made my way to the head of the table, avoiding any obstacles or booby traps in my way. (The evil cocktail fork still lay, sharp tines up, on the floor.)

Then suddenly I wasn't the center of attention anymore. What seemed like hundreds of waitstaff carrying dishes of desserts swarmed the table.

I slipped gratefully into my new seat, as the prince stood and held it out for me.

"The chair of honor, milady," the prince (THE PRINCE!!!) said.

Once again, near the prince, my brain shut down. I sat, mute, as pastries and puddings were laid out in front of me.

Belle to the rescue.

"Here are the many sweets we Brits enjoy," she told me. "They may not compare to a double-scoop sundae at Mimi's Creamees, but I hope they'll do."

I smiled and relaxed a bit, remembering all the good times we'd had at Mimi's back home in Lake George. "They look amazing," I said. "But I don't recognize anything."

"This is trifle with cream," Belle explained, pointing to a dish, "and here's castle pudding, elderberry sorbet, and chocolate banoffee pie."

Here I was, surrounded by some of the most famous faces in the world, but I only had eyes for that pie. And that's how my first dinner at Buckingham Palace ended. Seated between my favorite cousin and her handsome prince. Sweet. And yum, yum, and yum.

"Okay," Evie said. "Just tell me one more time. You got to sit up with the prince and Belle while Miss Snobby Wannabe was left behind?"

We were Skyping. It was awesome to see my best friend's face on the screen while we dissected my crazy day. I was psyched that she'd been available after her music lesson. Over there it was 5:30 p.m. Eastern Standard Time. Here it was 10:30 p.m.—just the right time to sink back into my silky bed, propped up with pillows and my laptop on my legs.

"Yep, that's exactly what happened," I sighed happily, probably still giddy from a sugar buzz.

"Ooh . . . I'll bet that Pandora was *fuming*," Evie said. "You may need to watch out for her. She doesn't sound like the type to take this sitting down. Oh—get it? Sitting down? Like on your fork!" she giggled.

"Uh, yeah, let's not go over that part again," I requested. I'd thought it over and could only come to one conclusion. Pandora had put that fork on my seat after I'd jumped up when she'd spiked my foot. Evie agreed it was sabotage. Pandora was out to get me.

"So anyway," I said, "after the dinner, when Belle and her bodyguard were walking me to my limo—"

"When the princess and her bodyguard blah blah blah blah *limo*," Evie interrupted.

"I know, I know, it sounds very . . ." I searched for the word. *Unlikely? Ridiculous for a small-town nobody?*

"Posh," Evie said. "It sounds very posh."

"Right," I nodded. "Anyway, Belle told me that they've arranged a tour guide to take some of us younger people around to see the sights of London. And guess who's on that tour?"

Evie drew a red heart on her computer screen. <3

"Very funny," I said. "Yes, him. Tristan. Evie, I wish you were here."

A cartoon mustache appeared on Evie's face.

"Stop goofing around with the graphics features!" I laughed.

"Remember," Evie said, the mustache vanishing. "You are there because Belle wants you to be there. And so far, it sounds like your special mission is going well, too. I mean, it was really cool of the prince to rescue you like that."

"Yeah," I admitted. "But it's been only one day. How's he going to be for the rest of their lives, till death do them part?"

"Evie! Have you finished your homework?" Suddenly, Evie's mom showed up on-screen with a stern look. "Evie, you have studying to do. Now. Hello, Claire. And good-bye, Claire."

"Good-bye, Claire," Evie echoed. I watched as she morphed her mother's face into a swirly, stretchy, distorted image. I totally cracked up. Then the screen went blank.

I yawned and shut my laptop down. What. A. Day.

After I'd left the dinner, I'd taken my limo to the luxurious hotel we were staying in. I'd spent the whole ride talking to my mom on the cell phone, describing what people wore, what the queen said to me (nothing), what foods were served, and every other detail I could remember. I hadn't told her about the fork incident or Pandora. My mother likes to hear about happy things and tends to filter out the rest. Thank goodness for Evie and video chat.

I went out into the suite to say goodnight to Mom. She was stretched out on a dove gray velvet couch and leaning on a silk pillow.

She was reading a book.

Wait.

My mother reads magazines, not books. Was England making her more cultured already? I moved closer, so I could see the title.

"*Royal Astrology*," I read aloud.

Mom looked up.

"The stars explain many of the royals' relationships." She shook her head. "So many of them had totally incompatible signs. What were they thinking?"

Um, that horoscopes don't mean anything?

"You'll be happy to know," Mom continued. "That Belle is a Capricorn and the prince is on the cusp of Cancer, which makes them a nice match," Mom told me.

Or maybe they do mean a little something?

At that moment, I realized that I wanted the prince to be as great as he seemed. I wanted to believe that he *would* make Belle happy. That he wasn't too good to be true. But I was too exhausted to think about the prince or the wedding or the dinner or *anything* anymore.

"Good night, Mom," I said, going over to her.

"Good night, Sweetie." Mom pulled me down for a hug and kiss. "I'm very proud of you."

"Thanks," I said, and went off into my bedroom with a nice, cozy feeling inside. And that feeling stayed with me as I got into the fluffy-comfortered bed with the pink-tulips-on-white print. There were *real* pink tulips in a crystal vase on the night table next to my bed, along with an alarm clock, which I set for the tour in the morning. I put my cell phone there to charge.

I was asleep the moment my head hit the feather pillow.

Zzz.

I was awakened the next morning by my cell phone. I felt around the night table and found the phone. I opened my eyes and looked at it. There was a text waiting for me.

C—Have fun on the tour! Me—pep
rally today. Woo and hoo. XOXO EV

Everything slowly sank into my morning brain. *I'm in London . . . fancy hotel . . .*
ROYAL WEDDING COUNTDOWN—THREE DAYS!

I jumped out of the snuggly bed and stumbled out into the main room of the suite.

"Mom?" I said. I looked around the suite. On a table I noticed a note propped up against a crystal vase of fresh yellow flowers.

Claire, I'm off to see the best of London! I was invited on a tour with some other out-of-towners. We're off to Picadilly Circus and Madame Tussaud's Wax Museum and to go shopping! Text me when you wake up.

Mummy

Mummy? I went to sleep with a Mom and woke up with a Mummy? Oh-kay. I looked at the clock.

Yeeps!

I was supposed to meet the tour guide in the lobby in eleven minutes! I quickly shoved a muffin from a basket on the table into my mouth and texted my mom, "good morning." Then I raced back into my room to get dressed.

Exactly ten minutes (and one more muffin—these British baked goods are total yum) later, I stepped off the elevator at *L*. Standing in the lobby was a tall Asian woman with a sign that said "Claire-Bear." With a drawing of a teddy bear.

Ooh, I'm going to get Belle for this! I certainly hoped none of the other kids on the tour saw that sign.

"I'm Claire," I said.

"Pleasure," the woman said, smiling. "My name is Daphne, and I'll be your tour guide today." She flashed an ID at the man standing guard at the revolving door. He let us through to the outside.

"I'm a student at Oxford," Daphne said, after we had revolved our way to the sidewalk. "Also, Belle was my minder, watching me when I was a tot."

"Really?" I said. "Belle was your babysitter? Was she a good one?"

"Mostly," the tour guide said. "She was fun, but she made me eat my brussel sprouts. Gak."

I decided I liked Daphne. Especially when she said, "Welcome to the deluxe tour" and pointed to a red double-decker bus.

"We're taking a red double-decker bus?" I squealed.

"Hey, Claire-Bear!" I heard a boy's voice shout from above. I looked up. Tristan was calling out from a window on the top deck of the bus. "Come aboard!"

Okay. I didn't know if I should be mortified at being called Claire-Bear or excited to see Tristan.

"Step on in," Daphne said, and we got on the bus.

"Oi'm Gus, and Oi'm in charge of this 'ere bus," a bald man sitting in the driver's seat said.

"Thank you, Gus," I said.

"It's a lurvely day for a jaunt." Gus smiled at me. He had a nice smile but bad teeth. "So go on up with yer mates, and we'll be off!"

"Thank you, Gus," Daphne said. We walked halfway to the back of the bus, passing empty seats.

"Where are all the people?" I asked.

"Oh, the Palace ordered a private tour," Daphne said. "There's just the four of you. Everyone else has been picked up, so let's meet them up on the top, shall we?"

Daphne climbed the stairs that led to the top. I followed her.

I had a happy shiver. This was real! I was touring London on a private, red double-decker bus!

And then I saw Pandora. She was head-down over her cell phone, tapping at the keys.

Ergh. If that girl bugged me, I would just go down to the first level. And hopefully Tristan would come down with me. And we could be sort of alone!

I spotted Tristan sitting on the opposite aisle from Pandora. Then I noticed he was not alone. Sitting next to him, rather closely, was a girl. A girl with long, straight red hair with gold highlights, wearing a cute green knit cap and green Wellies.

The girl turned to look at me, and my heart sank. She was pretty, in a natural, casual-chic sort of way. And she was smiling, happily seated next to Tristan.

Time to face reality. I was here for Belle's romance, not mine.

Sigh.

(Letter dated one year ago)

Dear Claire-Bear,

You asked in your last letter if dating the prince was worth all the drama. I have had to do a lot of thinking about that question.

Love can be messy and complicated. When your love is in the public eye, all the complications are magnified, examined, distorted, judged. It sometimes seems that my relationship belongs to the world.

But it is also a place of peace, quite

separate from the outside. Love can be simple—two people who make each other better and stronger and happier.

Thank you for being concerned about me. When you're old enough and ready to start dating, I'll probably fuss all over you. That boy will have to be pretty special to get my stamp of approval.

In the meantime, just stay true to yourself and relax. Love will come when it's meant to. For me, it came in the form of a kind, funny guy who happens to be a prince. I'm glad you asked me that question. My answer—yes, he's worth it!!!

XOXO

Belle

Here I was. Just standing on the second deck of a double-decker bus. Yep. This was really, really awkward. I'd gotten on this bus all excited to see London and—okay—to see Tristan. But now it was like I was back in the lunchroom at school, holding my tray, feeling like everyone was watching me, and I didn't know where to sit.

Back home at school I could hide out in the girl's bathroom. But this wasn't school.

"Hi, Claire!" The red-haired girl next to Tristan jumped up and waved to me. "Sit over here next to me! We saved you a seat on the end, so you can see the views best."

Well, Tristan's girlfriend was really friendly. I forced myself to smile and sat down in the little chair next to the girl.

"Claire, this is Thalia," Tristan said with a grin. (*Ignore. Cute. Grin.*)

"So, Thalia, Tristan," I said, "How long have you two known each other?"

Thalia looked at me funny.

"All my life," she said.

"I told Mum and Dad that I wanted a puppy," said Tristan. "But they brought home a baby sister instead."

"Oh," I said. *Oh!*

"We don't look anything alike, do we?" Thalia said. "I favor our tall, ginger-haired father, while Tristan takes after our dark-haired, short Mum—"

"I'm not short," Tristan interrupted.

"Stand up and prove it," Thalia challenged. "I am only a couple centimeters shorter than you, and you're three years older."

"That's because you're a giraffe," Tristan said mildly. "If only they'd listened to me and brought home the puppy . . ."

Thalia whacked him on the arm.

"Greetings and salutations," Gus's voice boomed. I looked around and spotted a pair of loudspeakers on either side of the rows of chairs. I also noticed that Pandora was still texting.

"Oi'm Gus, and this is my bus, heh-heh," the voice continued. "Please buckle up. I am honored to drive you around our majestic city."

The bus engine roared to life.

"Thank you, Gus," another voice announced. "This is Daphne, and I'll be narrating your tour. After a brief jaunt, we will be stopping and disembarking at our first site."

The bus pulled away from the curb, and we were off! On the wrong side of the road, which still felt really weird.

"You're his *sister*," I said, and smiled to myself. *Hee. Yay.*

"What's funny?" Thalia asked.

"Um." I thought fast. "I couldn't help but think about all the kids back in my middle school stuck inside at their desks. And here I am out in the London air on a double-decker bus."

"The London air is rather smoggy," Thalia pointed out.

"Thalia!" Tristan rolled his eyes.

"Just saying," Thalia said. "Anyway, what's your American school like? What are the American kids like? What year are you in school? I skipped two grades, so I'm only a level behind my brother even though he's thirteen and I'm ten."

"You're ten?" I asked, surprised. I'd thought she was older.

"Ten and a half, actually. Most people think I'm older because I'm tall and have a high IQ," said Thalia.

"Ladies and gent!" Daphne's voice came through again. "Please take a look to your left. You will see the spectacular St. Paul's Cathedral, which was designed by the famed architect Sir Christopher Wren. It was built after the Great Fire of 1666, which destroyed the entire city."

Wow. I'd read about that fire, but now that I was actually in London, it was hard to imagine. But that cathedral was cool. I held up my cell phone and snapped a photo of it. I texted a quick message to Evie and sent it, along with the photo, to her.

"Who is EV?" Thalia asked, looking over my shoulder. "Your boyfriend?"

"Thalia!" Tristan said. "Don't be so nosy!"

"EV stands for Evie, my best friend at home," I told her. "And, um, I don't have a boyfriend."

"Why not?" Thalia persisted. "American boys are s-o-o-o . . ."

Not interested in someone like me? I finished her sentence silently. And quickly changed the subject.

"Where's Callum?" I asked. And then regretted it. Callum was in a wheelchair. Maybe today's tour wasn't handicapped accessible, and Callum had to miss it.

"The computer program tracking the wedding's seating arrangements had a glitch, so the Palace called Callum."

"Excuse me?" I snapped out of my thoughts.

"Callum's the computer whiz," Tristan said. "He called and told me he had to fix the online wedding planner."

"Yes, imagine," Thalia giggled, "if the wrong people were seated next to each other. Like women who were angry with one another—or presidents of enemy countries."

"Well, we all know where we will be during the ceremony." Pandora walked over and sat down in an empty seat in the row in front of us, turning around to face us. I guess she was done texting and avoiding us. So why was she sticking her snooty nose into our conversation now? "Except for you, Thalia. Where will you be?"

"Mum and Dad and I are hosting our own party," Thalia said. "With a huge screen TV and catered food."

"What?" I was startled. "You're not going to be at the wedding, Thalia?"

"She wasn't invited," Pandora smirked.

"You don't have to be so mean about it," Thalia said quietly.

"Pandora, you know it's not personal, it's protocol," Tristan said.

"Wait!" I frowned. "I'm totally confused. How come you and Callum and Pandora made the guest list? And not Thalia?"

"Here is our first stop," Daphne's voice boomed. The bus pulled over to park. "Please come down and meet me at the exit door."

"I'll explain it all to you later," Tristan said to me.

Woo-hoo! Thus insuring a future conversation with the Cute Boy!

"Thanks," I said, blushing. I followed everyone down the stairs from the upper deck to the lower level, where Daphne was waiting.

"Let's get on with it, shall we?" Pandora said. "I've got a schedule to keep." (She said "shed-ule.")

"If you're going to be so miserable," Thalia said, "why did you even come today?"

"Because the prince told my aunt about it, and of course our families are so close, she thought it was a good idea. Anything to make the prince happy."

"Yes, well, hopefully you will get something out of it," Daphne said briskly.

"Blisters," Thalia said. We all looked at her. "She'll get blisters on her feet out of it."

I tried not to laugh at Thalia's bluntness. Pandora was wearing high-heeled black boots over black skinny jeans. Her winter-white coat looked suspiciously like one I'd seen on Belle in photos. Pandora was not dressed for a tour. With her silky black hair pulled back in a black velvet headband and her red lipstick, she looked like she was expecting someone important to see her.

Not just us.

Pandora pushed past all of us and got off the bus first. "Pandora," Daphne called, exiting next, "rule number one—stay with the group."

"I could be wrong," I said, stepping down the exit stairs, "but Pandora doesn't strike me as the rules-following type." I heard Thalia giggle behind me.

And then we were all off the bus, looking up at our first stop on the tour. "She might want to behave herself here," Tristan said quietly. "This place hasn't treated misconduct too kindly."

"Welcome," Daphne said grandly, "to the Tower of London."

11

Mom—Remember my Rapunzel phase? I tried to grow my hair long and hang it down off our balcony, pretending I was up in the tower. C

C—how cld I forget? I had to call Claire, Claire, let down your long hair over + over. Mum

P.S. Just got my pic taken with Johnny Depp, Beyonce, and Brangelina! The wax ones—ha ha.

"Greetings!" said a guard as we walked through the entrance gate of the Tower of London. He was wearing a blue coat with red trim, and a top hat.

"Pass on through," he waved. "But enter at your own risk! Many have entered, but not all have exited."

We walked a bit, and then . . . WOW. A massive stone tower rose up from the ground, surrounded by walls and buildings. There were many people walking around, looking as amazed as I felt.

"It looks like a beautiful medieval castle!" I said. But I knew that it had a much uglier history.

"Prison, fortress, torture chamber, execution site," Tristan said in a spooky voice.

"Shush, you're creeping me out!" Thalia swatted him good-naturedly.

"Tristan's correct," Daphne said. "This place has been all those things and more. The guards here are known as Beef-eaters, and they traditionally warn visitors who pass under the Bloody Tower."

"It sounds like a place for Death Eaters, not Beefeaters," Thalia joked.

"Are we almost there?" Pandora whined. She looked wobbly. Probably because her stiletto heels weren't exactly the wisest fashion choice.

"Actually, we are here," Daphne said.

We stood among a small crowd.

"This is the scaffold site," a Beefeater leading a tour announced. He began telling us about the executioner's block that used to be here, and the people whose heads were chopped on this *exact* spot.

And we were here, hundreds of years later. We were standing on history.

The guard stopped talking. I looked up.

OMG. I was standing on history. Alone.

I mean, there were still other tourists, but not one of them was someone I knew.

Where did everyone go?

Do. Not. Panic. I'm going to panic!

And then I saw Pandora! I never thought I'd be so happy to see that girl. She was walking quickly, tripping on her heels into one of the buildings. I ran after her.

She must be trying to catch up with the group.

I weaved in and out of people and followed where Pandora had gone. I went inside and looked around. More people, some heading up stairs. I climbed the stairs, figuring everybody would be up there.

I figured wrong. Only Pandora was up there. I saw her through a gap in the crowd.

"Pan—!" I stopped in the middle of yelling her name. Pandora was standing with an older woman. She looked familiar. . . .

Then I remembered. It was the secretary who'd barged in on Mags and me, when I was getting ready for the royal dinner.

Miss Cornelia! That was her name. What in the world was *she* doing here?

I squinted. It looked like Miss Cornelia was spritzing something from a small bottle onto Pandora. A mist sprayed out all over her hair. Miss Cornelia waved her hands around in circles, squirting and spritzing. Miss Cornelia was here to spray perfume on Pandora? *Whuh?* This made no sense.

Then Pandora suddenly turned and began walking in my direction. *Eeps! Should I hide?* Obviously they were meeting secretly, and I didn't want Pandora to know I saw her. I decided the safest answer was yes. I scrunched up against a wall, flattening myself as best I could. Fortunately Pandora didn't see me, and she headed downstairs.

"Excuse me, miss, you're blocking the exhibit," a short round man with a short round boy said to me.

"Oh." I stepped away from the wall, careful to not let Miss Cornelia spot me. "Sorry."

"Look Dad," the boy said. "Medieval graffiti! And blood-stains! Awesome!"

I looked at what I'd been leaning against.

Okay. That was creepy.

Which reminded me—where was Miss Cornelia? I spotted her coming slowly through the crowd.

"These were the desperate final messages of the doomed prisoners," a guard was saying. "Carved with bone, marked with blood."

I fled. Down the stairs, out the exit, back into the court-yard, past all the people, and—*wham!*—I ran smack into Tristan.

"Tristan!" I was so happy, I hugged him. Then I froze. Because I was hugging the cute boy I was crushing on.

Awkward.

Then the coolest thing happened. He wrapped his arms around me and hugged back!

"Claire! What a relief! Are you all right? Somehow we lost you and Pandora," Tristan said.

I blocked out the name "Pandora" for a moment and just enjoyed the hug.

"Come on," said Tristan, as we both stepped back away from each other at the same time. "I'll take you to where Daphne and Thalia are waiting."

"My hero!" I (not really) joked.

Tristan held out his hand to me. "Milady," he said grinning.

I put my hand in his, and we walked through the court-yard. Together.

(Letter from two years before)

Dear Claire-Bear,

Remember the bracelets we made by braiding colored threads? We wore them on our wrists and ankles and in our hair. I think of it as Lake George jewelry. Well, you may have noticed in photos of me in the magazines that my adornments have changed. I'm half dazzled and half terrified to be wearing pearls and rubies and sapphires. They are loans from jewelers who wish for publicity, so while I feel like

a walking advertisement . . . I also feel
like a queen!
   XOXO
   Belle

"Here you will see the crown that the queen wears for official functions," a Beefeater told us, "It has 3,733 jewels . . ."

"I want one," Thalia whispered to me.

I giggled. I was so relieved to be back safely with my group.
Tristan had brought me to the crown jewels, where Daphne
and Thalia were. Pandora had also beaten me there. I was
pretty confused. How did she know where everybody had
gone? And, more importantly, what had she been doing with
Miss Cornelia?

I didn't get any answers, because we were hustled onto a
moving walkway, which took us past display cases of glitter-
ing ceremonial accessories, like jeweled swords and staffs and
then . . . WOW! The crown jewels! Spectacular crowns with
ginormous diamonds and hundreds of other gemstones.

I temporarily forgot everything around me, so dazzled I was
by the jewels. I was like a little kid distracted by shiny things.

But then our tour was over, and we stepped back out into the gray London Tower yard. As we lined up to board the double-decker bus, I made sure to stand behind Pandora. I leaned forward slowly, getting close to Pandora's head just as she raised her hands to smooth out her hair.

"Ow!" I said, as I got smacked in the nose. Pandora whirled around.

"What are you doing?" she demanded, frowning.

What could I say? *I'm sniffing your hair, because I saw an old woman spray you?*

Uh, no.

"Sorry, a bit clumsy," I managed. My voice sounded funny, as I was still holding my wounded nose. Which, I realized as we boarded the bus, I was now unable to smell with.

On the second deck, Pandora sat right behind Daphne and immediately began texting. Since I couldn't find out any more about that weird meeting, I decided to put it out of my mind.

And guess who I put *in* my mind? Tristan. Duh. I sat down next to Thalia, who was by the window, and tried not to stare as her brother came our way down the aisle.

Sit here, sit here, sit—yes!

Tristan sat down on my left, in the aisle seat. I was happily in the middle.

"So, Claire," Thalia said. "Tell us about the fabulous parties you attend in the States."

Um, did she think I walked the red carpet at celeb events in Lake George?

"Well, I was hoping I could ask you two a question," I said. "How do you know the prince and Belle?"

"I can answer that," said Tristan, his eyes making me feel melty.

"When I was a first-year student at prep school, I was assigned an older mentor, like everyone else in my class. Someone to guide me and also to have my back. Then I found out my mentor was the prince. Of course, I had to play it chill, but as a first-year brat I had hit the jackpot. Not because he was a prince, but because he was such a great guy."

"I, of course, went totally bonkers," Thalia added.

"The prince wasn't *in* school anymore, but he had to do service hours during his stint in the military, so he thought he'd mentor at his old alma mater," Tristan went on. "I was chosen because we had a common interest—military history.

And we're both fans of the same football team."

"Football . . . that's soccer, right?" I asked.

"Americans call it soccer," Tristan said, nodding. "Do you follow it? Do you play?"

"Um, no," I told him, trying to think of something soccer-related to impress him. "I know about Beckham."

"Oh, dear." Thalia grinned. "Now you've done it."

"Beckham! How come Americans only know one player?" Tristan said. "Football is so much bigger than one bloke."

"One incredibly handsome bloke," Thalia sighed, "who will be at the royal wedding with his fabulously stylish wife!"

"Really?" I looked at Thalia. Cool. I knew that celebrities would be attending—which was exciting but also made me even more nervous. What if I got starstruck and made a fool of myself?

"Girls," Tristan said, "you are missing the point. I was saying how the prince and I are fans of the same team, which is another reason we get on so well."

"Boys and football," sighed Thalia. "I don't get it."

"A lot of girls play soccer at home," I said. "And our U.S. team is awesome. I'm just not very sporty."

An understatement, considering I was usually picked last in gym class.

"Well, I'd be happy to tell you more about it." Tristan smiled at me. "Especially if you root for the right team."

"I'll consider it." I smiled back. OMgosh, he had a great smile. Was I blushing? My face felt hot. Yep. I was blushing. "Uh—er—," I stammered. What had we been talking about? Brain freeze!

"Claire, is your cousin wildly nervous about the wedding? You're so lucky to be related to her! She's s-o-o-o beautiful and she seems so lovely. Is she truly as nice as she seems? Are you two quite close?" Thalia bounced up and down in her seat as she peppered me with questions.

"Yes, Belle is super nice," I told Thalia, relieved to sound normal again. "And we have an amazing relationship."

"I think the prince is very lucky," said Tristan. "Your cousin is splendid, Claire."

Oh-kay. That was really, really nice. This boy was more than just cute.

"Well, you and the prince must have gotten close, if he asked you to be in the wedding party," I said.

"Yep, he says I'm the younger brother he never had," said Tristan.

"Hey!" I exclaimed. "That's what Belle says about me! I mean, 'little sister,' of course."

Tristan and I smiled at each other.

"Well, I'm the little sister Tristan *does* have," Thalia said. "And quite lucky for him. Somewhat unpleasant for me, however. Claire, do you have brothers?"

"No," I answered, but I was cut off from further talking because Tristan had leaned over me and started tickling his sister.

"I'm unpleasant, eh?" Tristan said.

Thalia shrieked and squirmed. They didn't seem to notice me getting squashed in the middle.

"I take it back!" Thalia squealed. "Stop already!"

Tristan stopped and sat back in his seat. "So, I'll tell you about the rest of us," he said calmly, as if our conversation hadn't been interrupted by a sibling tickle attack. "Callum's family and the prince's family go way back generations. And Pandora is the grandniece of the queen's husband's secretary."

"Errg!" Thalia shuddered. "Please let's not talk about her great-aunt Cornelia."

"Shh," Tristan said. "Don't be too rude. Or too loud." He gestured toward Pandora.

"Wait," I said quietly. "Did you say her *great-aunt* Cornelia?"

So it was Pandora's great-aunt who was spraying her at the Tower of London? That still didn't make any sense.

"Yes," Thalia said, shuddering again. "But I don't want to talk about her anymore."

Strange. I wanted to know more, but . . .

"Look out the window, everyone!" Daphne called. "We are crossing the river and almost at our next destination."

"I wonder where we're going," Thalia said, sounding happy to have the subject changed.

"Well, wherever it is," Tristan said, "be prepared to see your cousin's face everywhere, Claire."

"I know. I still can't get used to it," I admitted.

Everywhere I'd been today—from the hotel lobby to the tower to the sidewalks, people were wearing royal wedding gear. T-shirts, caps, pins, shoes—even their souvenir bags featured Belle's and the prince's faces. Inside those bags could be Belle and Prince action figures or spoons or mugs or flags or coins. The merchandising was unbelievable.

I was trying hard to ignore it and focus on my *cousin* Belle, not Belle the princess bride. Pretty hard to do when versions of her were staring me in the face everywhere I looked. Larger-than-life, perfectly Photoshopped Princess Belle, reminding me how imperfect I was. I couldn't help comparing the wedding the British people expected to the real-life wedding with me in it—clumsy, unroyal, small-town me.

My recurring panic set in. What if I accidentally ruined the wedding???

"Claire, are you all right?" Tristan asked.

Not really. I took a deep breath and managed a weak smile.

"Sure," I said to Tristan. Oh, he was so cute when he was concerned. So. Cute. I started feeling much better.

"I think your cousin is handling everything extremely well," Thalia said. "It's like a carnival out there, but she's as poised as ever."

I smiled a real smile. Thalia was so nice, too. It felt like I'd made a new friend.

"You should tell her that," I said.

"Oh! I've never met her!" Thalia exclaimed. "I've only met the prince."

"Belle would love to meet you, I'm sure!" I told her. "I'll tell her about you. I just know she'll arrange something. It'll have to be after the wedding, though. Is that okay?"

"Okay?" Thalia's eyes grew wide. "It would be like a dream!"

Wow. It was weird—good weird—to be able to make someone's dream come true. This new London version of Claire, riding a double-decker bus with new friends, was pretty surreal. Every moment was so unexpected. I never knew what would happen next!

"We've arrived!" Daphne announced, as the bus came to a stop.

I looked out the window. Maybe I did know what would happen next. I recognized where we were. I'd been singing about it since preschool—well, before I ever imagined I would see it in person. The famous London Bridge!

ROYAL WEDDING COUNTDOWN:
Three Days

Hi EV! Look! London Bridge is not falling down! Can you see it behind us? ☺ C

Click!

Daphne, the tour guide, snapped the picture. "Quite nice," she pronounced. "Let's take a quick look-see around before proceeding to our next destination."

Daphne handed my cell phone back to me. I checked out the photo. Three people, in front of the *real* London Bridge. Me, Tristan, and Tristan's sister, Thalia.

Pandora was standing farther down the riverbank, away

from the rest of us. It looked like she was texting again. That was fine with me. I didn't want Pandora's face on my phone screen anyway. Thalia? Yes. Tristan? YES!!!

"Okay! Please turn your attention here," Daphne said. "This statue of a winged lion stands guard over the city. It is called a griffin."

"Like Gryffindor?" Thalia said excitedly.

"My sister is a Harry Potter nut," Tristan said to me. *He's looking at me. He's so cute!!!* I felt myself blush. I held up my camera and took a picture of the griffin.

"The staircase next to it," Daphne continued, "was the setting of a notable scene in Charles Dickens's *Oliver Twist*."

"Hey!" I said. "We saw that movie in English class!" And then I did something really dumb. I sang a line from the movie. "Food, glorious food!"

Yeeps. I shut my mouth. Now everybody knew I was a doofus. And that I had absolutely no singing talent.

"Oh, don't remind me of food," Tristan groaned. "I'm starving!"

"He's *always* hungry." Thalia rolled her eyes. At least no one mentioned my singing.

"We'll get a bite to eat at Borough Market," Daphne said, "after we visit Shakespeare's Globe."

"Finally," Pandora said, coming over to join the rest of us. "Some culture. Shall we go ahead and board the bus?"

"Actually, the bus is parked and will be available when we need it—which is not right now," Daphne said. "We will be walking, as it is such a lovely day."

Really?

I looked at the sky. Gray. Cloudy. It was chilly enough that I wore a jacket. And my new Wellies. I loved my boots.

"This is considered excellent weather for London at this time of year," Tristan said. "In April, you never know. There might have been a thick fog or rain or snow or gusty wind."

"The day's still young." Daphne smiled. "London weather is so unpredictable; it can change by the hour."

"Say, Tristan," Pandora said. "Who made you the expert on London anyway? You're not even from here."

"You don't live in London?" I turned to Tristan in surprise.

"No, we live in the Yorkshire Dales," he said.

"And Pandora lives there, too," Thalia added.

"I spend so much time in the city," Pandora said. "We consider the Yorks our country home."

Thalia snorted.

"Friends, Romans, countrymen, lend me your ears!" Daphne said suddenly.

"Er—what?" I asked.

Pandora gave a loud sigh. "It's Shakespeare," she said, rolling her eyes.

"And this," Daphne said, "is Shakespeare's Globe!"

I looked at the round building. *Wow.* William Shakespeare watched his plays being put on right here.

"This is actually a replica of the original theater," Daphne said. "The real one burned down during a play in 1612. That one was located a couple hundred meters that a way."

Okay. Shakespeare watched his plays over *there.*

"We'll have a short tour inside," Daphne told us. "There are no performances till summer, but there are exhibits to see—all about Shakespeare's world."

"All the world's a stage," I said, holding up my cell phone and taking a photo. I wanted to send it to my father, who'd had bit parts in Shakespeare's plays.

"What?" Pandora said. She was staring at me with a strange look on her face.

"It's Shakespeare," I said. *Ha.*

"*Finally,*" Pandora said, under her breath. Then I realized Pandora wasn't staring at me, but at something else. I turned to look.

O. M. Gosh!

It was the prince! Walking down the street with some large men I assumed were his bodyguards.

Other people around us on the street looked too. I heard them saying, "It's him!" "It's the prince!"

And then Pandora suddenly bolted away from our group, her heels tap-tapping on the street. She was running straight toward the prince!

"Yoo-hoo!" she called, waving wildly.

"Oh dear," Daphne said. "She knows we're supposed to stay close together. Follow me, guys." She walked briskly after Pandora, and we followed.

Then something really weird happened. A young, very pretty woman walked by the prince. As the woman passed by, the prince did a double take, looking once and then looking back again. He turned around and began to follow her.

Pandora stopped in her tracks. We all caught up with her just as the prince reached the girl. The prince took the girl's hand, and she smiled at him. And then, they embraced!

"Take a photo!" Pandora said. I realized I was still holding up my cell phone.

"Or I will," Pandora said. I realized I was not holding up my cell phone anymore. Pandora was! She snapped a photo of the embrace and then—even worse—another one of the prince kissing the young woman on the cheek! And then one *more* picture when the prince kissed her other cheek!

Was the prince a cad? A cheater? A flirt? Oh, poor Belle! This wasn't good.

"This isn't good," Daphne muttered. "Okay. Head count. Claire, Tristan, Thalia, Pandora. Please turn around and walk back toward the bus."

"But we didn't see the inside of Shakespeare's Globe yet," Thalia complained. "I wanted to . . ."

Her words were drowned out as a bunch of people raced by us with cameras, taking pictures of the prince. Tourists and—uh-oh! Paparazzi!

"Stop!" I shouted. This couldn't go public! "Stop!" Everyone ignored me. In fact, everyone *trampled* me. I was knocked one way, then the other, and I almost fell.

"A-a-a-ck!" I yelled. Daphne grabbed my hand and tried to pull me away from the scene. Tristan and Thalia were caught up in the chaos, too. Pandora seemed to be posing for the cameras.

"Oi'm 'ere!" Gus the bus driver was running toward us.

"Back off!" he growled to the people nearest us. "Police!" he said, and led me and Daphne away. Tristan pulled Thalia along behind us. I heard Pandora whine, "But things were just getting interesting," but soon she was with the rest of us.

I looked back and saw a bunch of security guards usher the prince into a black car with the royal insignia on it.

Whew! The prince was okay. I was okay, too. But WOW, I couldn't imagine what it must be like to be famous. And mobbed like that all the time. Thank goodness for the prince's security.

And for Gus.

"Thank you," I said, as Gus walked our group back to the bus.

"It's just me job," Gus said.

"Bus drivers chase off paparazzi?" I said, confused.

"Gus is really an MP—military police," Daphne told me. "On royal security detail."

"I have my own bodyguard?" Pandora squealed happily.

"You have your own bus driver," Gus said firmly. "Now hop up, folks, so I can take you to your next desty-nation. Stay on the bottom floor, please." Tristan ushered his sister onto the bus.

"Wow," I said, boarding the bus. "Next we'll find out Daphne isn't just a college student but a secret agent."

I looked at Daphne, expecting her to laugh, but she didn't. She just gave me a mysterious look.

I followed Daphne up the stairs onto the bus. There, blocking the aisle, was Pandora. Using my phone. Wait! *Why was she using my phone?*

"Pandora!" I said. "What are you doing?" Pandora tapped a couple more keys and then looked up at me.

"Nothing, Claire," she smiled. "Want to sit in the back with me?"

"Uh—no thanks." I glared at her. "May I have my phone back now?"

"Of course," Pandora said, handing it to me sweetly. "I do apologize for taking it from you. I simply got caught up in the moment. Quite a shock." I didn't have to look at her to know she was faking it. Poser Pandora. She was worse than Fake Farrah.

"I need to be alone now, please," I said, and slipped into a front seat on the aisle near Gus. Daphne headed with Pandora toward the back, where Tristan and Thalia sat.

The bus pulled away from the curb, but this time I wasn't looking out at the busy street. I stared at the photos of the prince. They clearly showed that he had some kind of relationship with this girl. But to kiss her on the street, in public? It was totally inappropriate! What kind of about-to-be-married guy does that?

A guy who should not marry Belle.

I wanted so badly to delete the pictures, but I didn't. I saved them, put my phone on my lap, and thought about what I was going to do next.

No matter what I did, it looked like this might be one fairy tale that would end happily NEVER after.

EV—Check out these pix . . . what
do u think?

I hit send and hoped Evie would see my message and
respond ASAP.

One minute went by. I watched the time change on my
phone. Two minutes . . .

Nothing. I sent a mental message: *Evie! Text me!* Apparently, my psychic powers were nonexistent, because my
phone was silent.

I couldn't just sit and wait for those awful-terrible-horrible
pictures of the prince kissing another girl to make their way

across the Atlantic Ocean and hope that Evie got back to me. So I got up and walked toward the back of the bus. I met Daphne in the aisle. She was going to the front, so we scooched around each other.

"Where are we going next?" I asked our tour guide.

"I'm going to talk to Gus and we'll decide," Daphne told me. "I'll let you guys know."

"Thank you," I said. The bus lurched. I grabbed on to a seat back and steadied myself. Then I went to confront Pandora. She was sitting across the aisle from Tristan and Thalia.

"Pandora," I said. "What were you doing—oof!" The bus went over a bump. And I flew off my feet and landed sprawled out over Tristan's and Thalia's laps.

"Please," Tristan laughed. "Join us."

"Claire, I'm so happy you're back," Thalia said. "I've been *crazy* to ask you more about living in the States!"

"Uh . . ." I picked myself up. Too. Embarrassed. To. Talk. Then, we all heard the weirdest noise.

"*Mrrrow! Meeeoww!*" It sounded like a sick cat was hiding in my jacket pocket.

"Did you change my ringtone?" I demanded, looking at Pandora.

"I wonder what Daphne is doing," Pandora said, and got up and walked to the front.

I answered my phone, and the sick cat stopped meowing. "Hello?" I said, taking the seat Pandora had just left.

"Claire, it's Evie."

"Evie! I'm s-o-o-o glad you called me back! Now, tell me what you think—"

"Hi, Evie! I'm Thalia!" Thalia yelled very loudly.

"Thalia!" Tristan tried to cover her mouth. The bus suddenly took a sharp turn and went over a bump, and I lost my grip on the phone, which bounced off my knee onto the floor.

Silence.

Then, "Claire! Hey! Are you guys there?" Evie's voice came loud and clear from the floor. *Whew!*

"I think you're on speaker!" I called to her. "Hold on. We're on a double-decker tour bus. I'm picking you up off the floor."

"Wow," Evie said. "This is the closest I've ever been to a double-decker bus."

"You're still on speaker," I told her, just so she wouldn't accidentally say something embarrassing about Tristan or anything.

"If Thalia's there," Evie said. "Is Tristan too?" *Uh-oh.*

"Yes, hello, I guess you've heard about me," Tristan said.

"Just the basics," Evie said casually. "Hey, Claire, leave me on speaker. I'd like to hear what you all think about those pictures."

"I—uh—sent the photos of the prince to Evie," I told Thalia and Tristan. "She won't say anything to anybody else."

"Evie!" Thalia shouted. "I'm thinking the prince has a secret evil twin—"

"Ladies and Gents," Gus's voice boomed over a loudspeaker. "We are taking a bit of a roundabout route in order to lose those paparazzi nutters. We will be arriving and deboarding at Buckingham Palace in five minutes."

"Okay, we already know Thalia's—um—creative interpretation," Evie said. "And I know we have only five minutes. Anyone else?"

"Putting my two pence in," Tristan said, "I think you might be making a big deal about nothing. A bloke greets a pretty girl. What's unusual about that?"

"What's unusual is that the bloke is the prince," Thalia said. "And the whole world is watching his every move."

"I've got to agree with Thalia," I said. "The prince is getting married in days! He shouldn't be risking his reputation so publicly." I continued, "And if the prince *is* sneaking around, shouldn't I give Belle the heads-up and protect her? She has bodyguards to protect *her*, but not her heart!"

"Or . . ." I felt fear rising inside me. "The bodyguards are on the queen's payroll! What if they're in on it? What if they do whatever the prince tells them to do?"

"Take a breath, Claire," Evie said. "Look, it wasn't a full-on kissing session, was it?"

"No!" I said. "I know, maybe I'm sounding a little crazy. But this does *not* help with my mission. I mean, I came here to find out if the prince and Belle were truly right for each other . . ."

"Claire?" Thalia tapped me on the shoulder. "I thought you came here to be a junior bridesmaid."

Oooooops. Did I just blow my secret mission?

"What Claire meant to say was that she's there to *celebrate* the prince and Belle being truly right for each other," Evie covered for me.

"Of course that's what I meant," I said.

Snort. The sound came from Pandora, who was on her way back to us.

"Pandora," Tristan said, "did they teach you that skill at princess camp?"

"Or pigness camp?" Thalia whispered to me, cracking up.

"Symonds," Pandora said. "You'd best leave me alone, if you know what's good for you."

"Ah, isn't that just what I said to you and Claudia Christopher when you tried to smooch with me in the schoolyard?" Tristan shot back good naturedly.

"That was back in nursery," Pandora said. "We were silly infants!"

"Oh!" Evie's voice broke into the squabbling. "I gotta go! Claire, I think you should keep quiet. Don't say anything to Belle. I mean, that girl could be an old college friend or even someone in town for the wedding!"

"You're right," I realized. Of the two of us, Evie was always the logical one. "Thanks, Evie! Miss you!"

"Miss you too—" Disconnected.

Okay. I would take Evie's advice. I felt calmer now and

realized the whole thing was none of my business, really.

Mrrrow! Meeowww!

Sick kitty phone. I answered it.

"Claire, it's Belle. What's this all about? Why did you send me these photos?"

"What photos?" I asked stupidly.

"The ones I just pulled up on my phone from you," Belle said. "Of my fiancé kissing a strange girl?"

"Oh! It wasn't me!" I gasped. "I didn't . . ."

"Buckingham Palace!" Gus called out. "All passengers off 'ere!"

"Yes, please, everybody come on up," Daphne said.

"Belle, you've got to believe me," I said into the phone. "It wasn't me!"

Nothing.

I looked. Dropped call. Belle was gone.

I thought about those photos. It *wasn't* me who sent them, of course. It was Pandora. Who was also gone. Off the bus and out of my sight. I hurried up the aisle and went after her. Not that I knew exactly what I would do when I found her. And I had to find Belle, too.

Suddenly, I heard a great noise from the other side of one of the wings of the palace. Cheers. Roars. Applause.

"They're changing guards," Daphne said. "Perfect timing. No one will notice us going in the servants' entrance."

So I followed her through an unmarked door. If I were a typical tourist, I'd be out watching the famous changing of the guards. Instead, I was slinking through a musty passage, freaking out.

Plantaganet, Lancaster, York, Tudor, Stuart, Hanover, Windsor . . .

Suddenly I realized I was IN the House of Windsor. And British history had just become real life.

15

Nothing.

I tried to text Evie, but fat chance getting any connection down in these winding corridors. Where were we—the basement? No, there weren't basements in a palace.

There were dungeons.

Ulp. Surely we weren't going to the dungeons. I mean, we'd messed up, but we weren't *criminals.*

"Uh, there aren't dungeons down here, are there?" I asked, my voice echoing off the cavernous stone walls.

"Don't worry." Tristan dropped back to walk beside me. "They haven't used the dungeons since—oh, the House of Stuart."

His English accent was s-o-o-o adorable.

"Right," I giggled nervously. "They could be brutal. Like, they beheaded their own king!"

"I didn't know you Americans learned British History," Tristan said. "Well done!"

"Oh, we don't. Not until high school anyway," I said, hurrying up to keep pace with him. "It's just an interest of mine, being related to Belle and all." *Wow.* I'd never been able to talk so easily to a boy. Maybe because it was pretty dark, and I didn't have to worry about how I looked. Then again, he was admiring my knowledge of history, not my appearance.

"We've arrived!" Daphne announced. Tristan and I were standing with Thalia and Pandora, who we'd found with Daphne in the lamplit hallway.

Arrived where? I thought, looking around at the stone walls.

"Ooh, I see a door!" Thalia exclaimed.

"Ooh!" Pandora echoed her sarcastically. "Maybe it's a *magic* door!"

Daphne pressed a button on the wall. A green light went on overhead, and the door slid open.

"The magic of modern technology," Daphne said. "Finger-print recognition."

"Okay," Tristan said. "Who are you *really?*"

"I'm a part-time student at Oxford," Daphne said, motioning us forward. "And a proud member of the royal security guard. Assigned to be your tour guide slash bodyguard."

"Cool," Tristan said. "Do you carry a gun?"

Daphne just smiled and stepped into the mystery room. I went in with the others and looked around.

"Cool," Tristan said again. The inside looked like a control room or something out of a sci-fi spaceship, complete with computer screens and boards with flashing lights. There were about ten people seated at the computers.

"Welcome to our lair," one of them said. He swiveled around in his chair.

"Callum!" Thalia said.

"Boffin, old boy!" Tristan went over to him, and the two guys did a fist-bump handshake greeting.

"Do we *have* to be here?" Pandora whined. "I have loads of important things to do."

The prince entered the room. Pandora changed her tone instantly.

"I mean, nothing is more important than assisting the royal family—oh, hello your highness!" She dropped into a perfect curtsy.

"Fakity-fake phony," Thalia muttered, as the whole room of people stood and bowed to the prince. Except for Callum, who nodded his head to greet him.

Formalities finished, the prince got to the point. "Now let's take care of this situation, shall we?"

A large screen had dropped down from the ceiling. An image popped up on it. It was the huge version of the photo taken from my camera. The one of the prince kissing the strange girl!

Wait.

I looked at the prince. What exactly did he mean by "taking care of the situation"? Was he planning a cover-up? Would he delete the proof and order us to keep quiet? I was American. I didn't have to obey him, did I? How could he possibly think I would keep secrets from Belle???

And then Belle came into the room.

"Hello, everyone," she said. "I came as quickly as I could!" She didn't look too upset . . . yet.

She hadn't noticed the picture blown up on the big screen. I wanted to give her a hug and tell her everything would be all right. I wanted *her* to give *me* a hug and tell me everything would be all right.

"Belle," I said. "I'm so sorry . . ."

"Pardon me," Daphne interrupted. "I just received a text, and I am needed upstairs. I'll be off then." She gave a brisk salute and left the room.

"I'd like to direct your attention up to the wall screen," Callum said. "You can see there is a young woman with the prince."

Oh-kay. Guess the secret wasn't quite so secret. But now what?

"Now," Callum continued, as if answering me. "Take a look at *this* photo, found in the archives."

Callum tapped on his computer, and the screen split, showing a different photo alongside the first. It was a newspaper photo showing the prince giving a balloon to a girl in a hospital bed. She was wearing a flowered hat to cover her bald head.

"Now watch this," Callum instructed. He zoomed in on the girl's face in both shots.

"It's the same girl!" Thalia squealed. "Just add the blonde hair!"

"Exactly," the prince said, looking at Belle. "I had to do a double take before I recognized her. And, before the gossip hounds made it look like something it wasn't, we issued this press release."

A document showed up on the screen.

"Claire," the prince said, not unkindly. "Would you please read it aloud for us?"

I squirmed and glared at Pandora, who was looking at the ceiling, like she had nothing to do with all of this.

"For Immediate Release," I read. "Fairy-Tale Reunion! Five years ago, sixteen-year-old Charlotte O'Malley was receiving a chemotherapy treatment at the London Free Clinic, when she was given the surprise of her life."

I stopped. I could see where this was going. I read on.

"'I could not believe the prince had come to visit,' the leukemia patient said afterward, awe still in her face. 'He brought me a teddy bear and a smiling balloon and wished me well. And he did the same for all of the ill children that day.'"

"Fast forward five years," I continued. "Earlier today

O'Malley and the prince coincidentally encountered each other on the Bankside. Charlotte O'Malley is now cancer free and, like the prince, engaged to be married.

Miss O'Malley, who still holds the teddy bear dear, was overjoyed to meet up again with the prince—this time under much happier circumstances. A fairy-tale ending, indeed."

The picture went dark. The room was silent. Only the whir of the screen rolling back up could be heard.

Then the workers in the room burst out into cheers and applause.

"Oh, darling!" Belle cried, flinging her arms around the prince. "We simply *must* send her flowers!"

"And," I ventured, "maybe a smiley balloon? She still has the bear, but she didn't mention the balloon."

"Brilliant," the prince said. "Yohan, please get on this right away."

"Yes, sir." A man began tapping madly at his computer.

"Thank you for reading that for us, Claire," the prince said, looking back at me. "I thought that since you were the one to notify us about the photo, you would like to announce the results."

"But, I wasn't . . . I mean, it *was* my cell phone but I

didn't . . . it was . . ." I tried to get the truth out, but—

"Ohhhhh!" We all heard a moaning sound and turned to look in its direction. Pandora was swaying back and forth and going, "I feel dizzy," and her eyes closed and then she started to crumple up and fall. The prince lunched forward to catch her, as he was standing nearest. But then *swoop*! Yohan the flower orderer got to her first.

Pandora sighed, "Oh, thank you!" And then she opened her eyes. "What are you doing?" Pandora suddenly regained her strength and jumped up from the man's arms.

"You were swooning, miss," Yohan said, backing away. "My wife does that sometimes if she has not eaten . . ."

"Oh, my goodness!" Belle said. "You all missed your lunch! You must be famished!"

"Yes, and it was because of me that your tour was cut short," the prince said. "Let us make it up to you kids."

I noticed Pandora grimace at the word "kids." But she *really* frowned when the prince spoke again.

"Pamela, we'll get some food into you right away."

Pamela? I'd thought Pandora said her family and the prince's were super close!

"We'll use the west kitchen," Belle was saying. "We can cancel our next appointment, honey. We *really* don't need to inspect the table coverings again."

"Yohan?" the prince said. "Cancel the table coverings meeting. My fiancée and I will provide a sumptuous, home-cooked meal. And because of what Cousin Claire did today, we'll make some American burgers! Please tell the chefs to deliver the necessary ingredients to the west kitchen."

"May we come too?" Thalia asked hopefully.

"Oh, that's not necessary," Tristan said. "You must be very busy." Thalia shot him a look.

"Oh, we won't take no for an answer," Belle said.

"Um—excuse me?" I said hesitantly. "What exactly did I do today?" *Besides looking like I'm spying on the prince and taking incriminating photos and sending them to show Belle that her fiancé could be kissing other girls?*

"You alerted us," the prince said. "Before the paparazzi could spread foolish stories, thanks to you we were able to get the truth out. So come along, Claire and Pamela, and you too, Callum. Geniuses need to eat also. And no arguments, Lord Tristan. You and Lady Thalia will dine with us, too."

Now, *I* felt dizzy. *Lord* Tristan? *Lord?*

"Don't think you're going to win." Pandora came up close to me and hissed in my ear. "It's far from over."

I looked at Pandora. She looked viciously angry, the scariest Mean Girl in the kingdom.

"Whatever," I said, shrugging. *"Pamela."*

16

"You're kidding me," Evie said through my cell phone. "Seriously?"

"I'm not kidding," I said seriously. "Seriously."

"Okay, let me see if I've got it," my best friend said. "Your tour was canceled because of paparazzi, the mean girl tried to sabotage you with your own cell phone but once again her plans backfired with you looking like the good guy—er—girl, and, speaking of guys, the one you're hanging out with is a lord?"

"Wow," I said. "You're a really good listener."

"Okay," Evie said. "I have only one question. Why is your voice so echoey?"

"I'm in a royal restroom," I told her. "It's the only place I could get reception." I waited. "Evie? Are you still there?"

"You're talking to me from a bathroom?" Evie finally said. "When you could be hanging out with the lord???"

"Um," I said. "You're making it sound like a religious thing."

That got us both cracking up. I was s-o-o-o glad I'd called. I always felt better after talking to Evie.

"I'd better go," I told her. "The burgers are probably about done by now. I need to make sure Pandora doesn't poison mine."

"Have you figured out what that girl is up to yet?" Evie asked. "Is she going after you, or Belle, or the prince?"

"I don't know what she's trying to do," I sighed. "Or why."

"Well, don't let her get to you," Evie said. "You've got more important things to think about. Oh, before you go, Claire?"

"Yeah?" I said, looking into the mirror over the sink. Everything in here was fancy and polished. Except me.

"Keep me posted?" Evie asked.

"Well, yeah," I said, applying a last swipe of lip gloss. "Meanwhile, would you do a search for 'Yorkshire Dales'?

Tristan lives there, and I don't know what the heck a dale is, so I was like, 'right, uh-huh, the Dales, of course . . .'"

I could hear Evie laughing as she hung up.

Okay. Time to get back out there and help Belle. I began to open the door, when I heard a voice in the hallway. *Her voice.* I froze, leaving the door open a crack, and listened.

"But it wasn't my fault the plan failed," Pandora was saying.

"Was the prince at the exact location I had scheduled for him?" an old woman's voice said.

"Yes, Aunt Cornelia," Pandora said in a little voice that didn't sound like the mean girl I knew.

"Well, it is a setback," the woman said. "But only a slight one. The Fates are on our side, my dear, and the outcome is assured. The commoner is no match against destiny!"

And then the old woman let loose a cackle that Gave. Me. Chills.

Go away, I pleaded silently. And they did. Pandora went one way; Aunt Cornelia went the other. I waited for a minute to make sure the coast was clear.

Plantaganet, Lancaster, York, Tudor, Stuart . . . , I chanted to calm myself, and then I got out of that bathroom ASAP. I found everyone, including Pandora, just down the hall in a large dining room, with chandeliers hanging from the ceiling and a long table covered with a pale yellow tablecloth, brighter yellow placemats, and two large crystal vases filled with—yep—yellow flowers.

"Claire, welcome to the Yellow Dining Room," the prince said, smiling at me. "Your cousin is cooking in the kitchen." He pointed to an open doorway. I hurried through it.

"Belle," I said when I found her.

"Here you are." Belle turned around from the stovetop, spatula in hand. "Claire, come and tell me if these look like authentic American burgers."

I still felt shaky. I went over and hugged Belle around the waist. She put down the spatula and hugged me back.

"Are you all right, Claire-Bear?" my cousin asked softly. "Did you find the loo?"

"Yes," I said even more softly. "But I really, *really* need to talk to you. *In private.*"

"Oh, good, they're cooked just right!" Belle said loudly. Then her voice dropped to a whisper. "I'll do what I can. Soon, I promise."

Okay. I felt a little bit better. Then I took a closer look at the burgers and felt a bit worse again.

"Claire's granddad always put them on a grill," Belle informed everyone. "But I think they're frying up nicely."

Crispy, fried meat slabs in a pan? *Um, yuck?* Of course I didn't say a word.

"Well done, darling," the prince said, carrying over a plate with a large loaf of bread.

I'll say, I thought. Any more "well done," and the burgers would turn black. I encouraged Belle to take them out of the frying pan and put them on a plate.

"Callum and I have set the table," Thalia called from the adjacent dining room.

"And the drinks are all poured," Tristan added.

"This kitchen is where the chefs cook for themselves and eat after they put on a dinner," the prince explained. "They cook the guests' meals upstairs in the main kitchen." He sat down at the long table. So did the rest of us, with Callum pulling his wheelchair up.

The prince sliced the bread (no hamburger buns in England?), and we all created our own burger sandwiches.

"A toast," Tristan said. (How grown up!) "To the soon-to-be-wedded couple. Happiness and good luck always." We all clinked crystal glasses filled with ice water. *Clink! Clink!* I couldn't help noticing Pandora's glass didn't actually touch anyone's.

The prince took a big bite of burger. I was about to do the same when there was a strange gurgling sound.

"Honey?" Belle looked at her fiancé. "Are you all right?"

The prince nodded.

"He doesn't look so good," Callum observed.

"Is he choking?" Thalia asked. "I could Heimlich him! I learned it in health safety class."

The prince shook his head no and continued chewing. Finally he gulped the bite down.

"Delicious," he said in a funny voice.

I bit into my burger on bread. *Ew. Yuk. Gak.* The fried patty was dried out and tasteless. I tried not to gag.

"Um, is this how it's supposed to taste?" Thalia asked, wrinkling her nose.

"Oh dear," Belle sighed. "Not another one of my cooking disasters."

Pandora spoke up. "In Princess Prep we learned to make shepherd's pie and fresh strawberry biscuits with cream."

"Say, those are two of my favorites!" said the prince. He took another bite of the dried-out burger.

"What a coincidence," Thalia mouthed to me.

"Don't eat that!" Belle swiped his plate away. "It's disgusting. You know I'm a horrible cook. *Why are you still eating?*"

"I don't want to hurt your feelings, darling," the prince said simply.

Wow. I was impressed. Again. He really seemed to put Belle and her feelings first.

Maybe it was finally time to trust him. Maybe he would be able to protect Belle and be a good husband even with the whole world watching. Maybe?

Knock knock. The door opened, and a line of uniformed staff walked in pushing carts and carrying platters. Our table was quickly filled with every type of food imaginable: fruits, vegetable salad, soups and—oh-yeah—desserts!

"You didn't think my cooking was the *only* thing you'd get to eat?" Belle laughed. And she had the burger plates taken away.

We all helped ourselves. I chose a fruit cup, green salad, chicken noodle soup, and a slice of chocolate cake. And a few different types of cookies. Lemonade, too. *Num num num.*

"Claire," Tristan said from diagonally across the table. "Try one of these blackberry jam tarts. They're splendid."

He held out a little pastry, so I could reach it. When I took it from him, our fingers touched. (Repeat. Our fingers touched!!!)

"Thanks," I said, blushing. "Mmm . . . it's good."

"I noticed you were sticking to a more traditionally American fare," Tristan said. "I thought you might need to broaden your horizons a bit."

"If it involves desserts," I said, "then my horizons are limitless." Everybody laughed, which made me feel good.

"Speaking of horizons," Pandora said, "at Princess Prep, we learned all about international travel etiquette. I can say 'Please get the prince more tea' in five different languages."

"Handy," Callum said. "Priya will be disappointed that she had to go to Dubai and miss all that."

"Who's Priya?" I mouthed to Thalia.

"His girlfriend," she silently responded, pointing to Callum.

"So, Pandora," Belle was saying. "Tell me more about your program. It sounds like fun!"

"Sometimes." Pandora sipped some water. "But it was a lot of hard work. Being a princess is serious business, you know."

"Well, good for you," the prince said. "I'm sure you'll be well prepared for your career or marriage or whatever your goal is."

"My goal?" Pandora said. "My goal is to be a princess." And she daintily dabbed her lips with a napkin. And then she smirked at me when the prince wasn't looking.

As I ate a lemony shortbread cookie, I tried to straighten my thoughts out. Pandora was obviously up to something no good. Seriously no good! And Great-Aunt Cornelia? She was in on it too. But I was the only one who seemed to suspect something.

That meant I was the only one to stop whatever they were up to. Could I do it by myself? Should I tell Belle, who was already stressed about the wedding?

And did Tristan notice when our fingers touched? Was it possible he . . . liked me?

Who was I—Nancy Drew, Girl Detective?

Aaaaack! My head was swirling.

And, apparently, so was my stomach. Because, while everyone finished their dessert, I felt something rising in my throat. *Don't do it, don't do it,* I silently begged my digestive system. Thankfully it listened. I didn't burp after all. *Whew!*

"BUURRP!"

That was *not* me. It was the prince! He smoothly said "excuse me" and added, "Did you know that in Japan it is considered polite to belch to show enjoyment of your meal?"

"I knew that!" Pandora exclaimed. "We learned about it at Princess Prep. Of course, then we all agreed we would never go to Japan. Or France, because you have to eat snails." She shuddered.

"Diplomatic relations would be very interesting if you were a princess," Callum noted.

"Thank you," Pandora said. "But you mean *when* I am a princess, not *if.*"

Oh. Kay. Everyone was quiet for a moment.

"Claire-Bear?" Belle said. "Would you please help me clean up the kitchen?"

For the first time in my life I was happy to clean. "Gladly," I said, and jumped up from the table, eager to get away from Pandora and finally talk to Belle alone.

17

ROYAL WEDDING COUNTDOWN:
Still Three Days

(Letter from six months ago)

Dear Claire-Bear,

Shhh! I have a secret! Of course, it won't be secret much longer, but for a little while I can share it with my most special people. Which includes you! So . . . He proposed!!! I'm engaged!!!

The ring is on my finger. And my hand feels so heavy. This is one very large rock of gorgeousness! It is an emerald of purest green, with many small but equally dazzling diamonds encircling it. Now I simply _must_ keep my manicures up-to-date.

(Remember the summer visit when I wore black nail polish to match my black wig? So fun!)

Anyway, we've agreed that our marriage (!) will be a modern one. I will not promise to "obey" or spend my life in the kitchen slaving away alone. We shall share household responsibilities, but honestly—as the future Queen (!!!)—I hope to publicly show how much I adore my husband and my country. It will be a balancing act of wife and royalty, but I can only do my best. I'm nervous and excited. Right now I can enjoy our vacation. (The safari was outstanding, and the people are so lovely. The insects and reptiles are frightful, however.)

XOXO

Belle

P.S. Would you please send me your grandma's recipe for tuna casserole? I think my fiancé would love it!

"We'll fill up the sinks so the dishes can have a good soak," Belle said loudly as she headed toward the kitchen. "That will give the cleaning crew a good head start."

"Grand idea!" the prince called after us. "We'll clean up out here."

"If I had servants, I'd *never* clean," I heard Thalia say.

"You never do anyway," Tristan teased her.

Then Belle turned on the faucets over the double sink, and everyone else was tuned out.

"Okay," Belle said. "No one can hear us. What's going on, Claire-Bear?"

I took a deep breath and let it out.

"Belle," I said. "There's something weird going on. Bad weird."

Belle looked at me and raised her eyebrows.

Okay. Where to start? "Who exactly is Miss Cornelia, Pandora's great-aunt?" I asked.

"Oh, she's been the queen's husband's social secretary for decades," Belle replied. "Everyone knows she's a bit dotty. I've never had a problem with her. Why do you ask?"

"Well, she seems to have a problem with *you*, Belle, and so does—"

"Pandora!" Belle interrupted me. "Thank you for bringing in more dishes. The sinks are still filling up."

"The prince requested your help with something," Pandora said. "Something to do with a spot of grease that is expanding over the linens?"

"Oh, dear," Belle said, and hurried away.

Drat!!!

"Allow me to help," Pandora said, grabbing a bottle of dishwashing soap. She started squirting a stream of it into the sink.

"Hey, we already put in soap," I said.

"Oh, this isn't like American soap," Pandora said. "You need to put much more in over here."

Wait, why was I standing here discussing cleaning methods with Pandora?

Then Pandora said in a low voice, "Bubble, bubble, royals in trouble."

"What are you talking about?" I said, grabbing the empty bottle.

"It's Shakespeare," Pandora smirked. "Sort of."

That's it, I thought. *I'm dealing with a crazy person.*

"All righty! Grease spot taken care of," said Belle as she came back into the kitchen. "Now, shoo, Pandora! You've been helpful enough already, and there's only room at these sinks for two."

Pandora exited.

"Hi," I sighed, and started putting some silverware carefully into the sink.

"So," Belle said quietly. "You were saying something about Great-Aunt Cornelia?"

"Yes!" I said, relieved to finally get to talk. "Something is going on with her and Pandora. And the wedding." Belle just looked at me.

Uh. What exactly should I say next that wouldn't upset Belle?

"I think they're out to get you!" I blurted.

Belle swished her hands in the water but didn't say anything.

"Do you think I'm being paranoid?" I asked. "I'm not making this up, honest!"

"Claire-Bear. Since when have I not trusted you? You've kept all my secrets and been on my side through ups and downs. Of course I will take what you've said seriously. Just as our guards take all threats seriously. And I can reassure you that we are all very protected. There's little chance anyone—a criminal mastermind, an elderly secretary, or even an admittedly irritating Pandora—could get in the way of our plans."

I sighed. Belle didn't get it. She was too bridally blissed out. I was on my own with this.

Belle was humming happily, scrubbing the silver, when suddenly . . .

"AAAAAAAAGH!" Belle let out a horrific scream. Her face turned pale.

"What?" I jumped.

The prince ran into the kitchen area, closely followed by Tristan and Thalia.

"What's the matter?" the prince exclaimed.

"Are you injured?" Thalia asked. "I know first aid!"

"No . . . it's . . . it's . . . look!" Belle held up her left hand. It took a moment; then I saw it. Or didn't see it.

"Your ring! It's gone!" I gasped.

"Quick! Turn off the faucets!" shouted the prince. "We'll search around in the water."

"You don't understand!" Belle wailed. "The bubbles were getting so high, I unplugged the drains. My ring may have gone down the pipes!"

"All right," the prince said. His cheeks were turning red, and he looked a bit worried himself. "Tristan, Claire, plug the stoppers back in. I'll call a handyman."

He whipped out his cell phone and spoke into it, while Belle flung herself into his arms.

Callum came in, his wheelchair barely making it through the door. "I heard," he said grimly. "Missing ring, open drain. One question. Why are the soap bubbles engulfing the room?"

"Omigosh!" I said. "Pandora squirted way too much dish soap into the sink! The drains are shut and there's nowhere for the bubbles to go!" Mounds of foam were expanding exponentially by the second.

"The handyman will be here in three minutes," the prince reported.

"We may be swallowed up by then," Tristan muttered. He waved some bubbles away from his face.

"I'm so sorry!" Belle burst into tears.

I stepped out of the room for a moment. It was too awful seeing Belle like this. Plus, I was gagging on a ball of bubbles. *Gak. Gak.*

"Looks like the ancestral ghosts are trying to untie the nuptial knot," a low voice said into my ear. "As my great-aunt Cornelia says, it's almost time for the dynasty's destiny to be restored to its true excellence."

"Pan—*gak*—dora (*choke, gasp*)!" I sputtered. "What did you say??? Why would you say that?"

"It's fate." Pandora grinned and flipped her glossy black hair behind her. "And you can't stop it." Pandora turned and walked out of the room. And she was gone.

I'd just barely gotten my breath back when I heard Belle sobbing. "Maybe it's an omen!" she wailed. *Oh no!* I raced back into the sink area.

"A what?" the prince was asking.

"A sign!" Belle cried. "That we're not meant to be married!"

Silence. No one said a word. Surely she wasn't serious?

Just then, Callum pushed his wheelchair up to the sink, pulling open the doors underneath, exposing the pipes. He reached into a bag on his chair and pulled something out.

A toolbox!

"What are you, a plumber?" Thalia asked. Her brother shot her a look.

"My wheels break down from time to time," Callum said. He turned on a flashlight, peered into the plumbing area and grabbed a wrench. "I always carry my tools."

"Thalia," he said. "Would you hold the light for me? Tristan, back me up with the tools."

Thalia took the flashlight and aimed it at the pipes. Then Tristan crouched down on the other side of Callum. Their huddle blocked my view.

The prince held Belle.

I held my breath. I heard a *squeak, squeak,* then . . .

SPLOOSH!

Water sprayed out from under the sink in all directions. Thalia and Tristan jumped back.

Whoosh!

We all shrieked as the water rained down on us. And bubbles. It was like being on the inside of a car wash. But with no car.

"I've got it!" Callum yelled triumphantly. *Squeak, squeak.* And the water stopped. "I've closed the pipes, but you might want to have a plumber check it because my wrench isn't too good—"

"Callum!" We all shouted.

"Oh, right," he said, and whirled around. In his hand was a long wire hook, bent at the end. With the ring on it!

"Hurray!" Thalia clapped.

"Woo-hoo!" I cheered.

"Callum, thank you!" Belle's tears turned to happy ones, as she let go of the prince and clapped her hands. "You're a hero!"

Callum's face turned bright red, and he mumbled something like "sokaynoprob." He held out the wire to the prince, who reached for it and took a step. Right into a puddle.

"Whoaaaa . . . !!!" The prince slid across the soapy floor like an out-of-control ice skater. On his way, he knocked into

Callum's hand, bending the wire back and then—*fling!*—the flawless emerald and diamond ring shot into the air, popping a few stray bubbles in its flight path.

Suddenly, Tristan leaped into action. He jumped in front of the prince, blocking him from sliding into the wall, and then reached up and caught the ring!

"He caught the ring!" I gasped. *Wow.*

Thalia rolled her eyes. "And yet he didn't even make the rugby team," she said. Then she paused. "Sorry," she said. "Sibling spat—bad habit. Nice going, big bro!"

We all agreed that Tristan, too, was heroic. Tristan just smiled and handed the now vertical prince the engagement ring.

"Belle," the prince said, *very* carefully walking across the floor toward her. "Even though I resemble a drowned rat and almost flattened myself against the wall and feel rather foolish at the moment . . . will you consent to be my wife?" He *very* carefully bent down on one knee.

"Awwwww . . ." Thalia and I said together.

"Well," my cousin said matter-of-factly, "even drowned rats need love. Yes, I would love to be your wife. Like I told you before. Remember? That safari trip we took?"

Then Belle began laughing, as the prince slipped the ring on her finger for the second time.

"I love you," she told her fiancé as he stood up and hugged her. Water droplets flew off both of them.

"And I you," the prince said back. *Awwww . . .*

"What in the name of the queen happened here?" A man walked into the room carrying a toolbox. Then he saw the prince and Belle.

"Oh, excuse me, Your Majesty," he said, bowing. "I was called to assist." He looked around, scratching his head.

"Long story, happy ending," Callum said. We all laughed.

Just then, both Belle's and the prince's cell phones went off. Belle took a look at hers.

"Oh no!" she gasped. "We're going to be late for high tea with the dignitaries. Sorry to rush out, everybody, but we must go right now!"

But, I thought, *we didn't get to finish our talk! People are trying to ruin the wedding!*

And now I could add Pandora's dumping all the dish soap in the sink to the other clues. Not that that proved anything.

But it was yet another weird drama Pandora had a hand in (no pun intended).

And what Pandora had said to me? Beyond weird. Oh, I was so confused. *What was I supposed to do???*

"Claire," Belle said. "I'll be in touch. Good-bye, everyone!" She grabbed the prince's hand, and they headed toward the door.

"I look like such a fright!" she wailed as they were leaving. "What will the queen say? What will my *mother* say?"

"Don't worry," the prince said. "I'll tell them it's all my fault."

And they were gone.

"Isn't that romantic?" Thalia sighed. "The prince taking the blame to protect his bride—even though it wasn't his fault."

"The prince is a stand-up guy," Callum agreed.

"Agreed," Tristan said. "Look at this place. We sure made a mess tidying up for the cleaning people."

"So, who put in the extra soap?" Thalia asked. "Belle? Or you?"

"It was neither one of us," I shook my head. "It was—"

"Pardon me," a man in a royal security uniform came into the room. "Is there a Miss Claire Gross here?"

"That's me," I said. Security? For me? Was I in trouble?

"I'm here to escort you to your car," the man said. "It will take you back to your hotel. As for the rest of you—your parents will be here momentarily."

"Oh," Thalia pouted. "We have to leave so soon?"

"Yes, miss," the security guy said. "Miss Gross, come with me, please." He spun abruptly and walked out the door.

"Um, bye?" I said to Thalia, Tristan (!!!), and Callum and hurried to keep up with Mr. Security Guard. I didn't have time to think as we wove through the hallways and through a door, and—just like that!—I was out of Buckingham Palace and in the back of a shiny black limo.

"Greetings!" the driver turned around. I recognized him as the chauffeur who'd driven me, my mom, and Belle from the airport.

It seemed like a long time ago. Back when my worries were all about messing up and making a fool of myself in front of the royal family and potentially millions of people. And making sure Belle was with Prince Right.

I still had those worries. But now there were even more things to be confused about.

I looked out the window and sighed. The people and buildings of London were whizzing by. I saw a billboard with gigantic faces of the prince and Belle. It said, "Celebrate with Crowne Cola!"

I leaned forward and popped open the mini fridge. Yep—a can of Crowne Cola. I took it out, opened it, and watched the foam pop out of the top.

Foam. Bubbles.

Okay. What had Pandora said while she was dumping the dish soap in the sink?

"Bubble, bubble, royals in trouble." Like she was casting a spell.

I shuddered. My imagination was starting to get the best of me. It was hardly possible for Pandora to know for sure that Belle's ring would slip off in the suds.

But what about her other spooky comments about the royal ancestors trying to keep Belle and the prince from tying the knot? And fate having other plans? There was no other explanation. Pandora wanted to stop the wedding. And her great-aunt Cornelia was in on it too.

I finished my soda pop as the limo pulled up to the hotel.

Would Pandora plus Cornelia plus fate equal no "happily ever after" for Belle and her prince?

I was so confused.

The chauffeur opened my door, took my empty cola can, and helped me out onto the sidewalk. I took a deep breath of London air and blew it out.

Okay. I'd tried to tell Belle, but that didn't work out. I doubted anybody else would believe my side of the story—except Evie, who was hundreds of miles away. And Thalia. She'd probably believe me! But she wasn't even invited to the wedding, so she couldn't help if things went awry. Besides, we were practically strangers to the royals. What could I possibly do in the face of the royal secretary who'd been trusted by the prince's family for decades? Not to mention her princess-in-training slash grandniece?

I was on my own. And I knew what I had to do. Stop Pandora! But how?

I had no clue.

18

Three Hours Later

Evie: Just checking in.

Claire: Wait till I tell you about my day.

Evie: Could it be more exciting than the spring concert? With my stellar clarinet solo?

Claire: Oh. Sorry. I forgot. It seems like everything is all about the royal wedding. Congrats on your solo.

Evie: Thx. But I was kidding. Everything IS about the royal wedding. That's all anyone talks about—on TV, online, at school.

Claire: At school?

Evie: Yeah. At least the girls are. Farrah's face is

like on every local news channel saying how she was in on the secret and you 2 are thisclose.

Claire: WHAT???

Evie: There's a spot waiting for you in the Poser Posse when you get back.

Claire: Ew!!! No thank you. I'm still anti-fakeitude.

Evie: Just saying. There's a ticket to the popular world here with your name on it.

Claire: I just threw up a little in my mouth.

Evie: Good. I mean yuk. But we're still besties?

Claire: Of course!!! Were you really worried?

Evie: Maybe

Claire: I'm still the same me. Your BFF. Who is freaking out about Pandora and ... OMG! Mom just came in and said there's a boy calling me on her phone!?! GTG

Evie: !!! Good luck !!!!

Claire: XOXO

I held out my hand for my mom to give me the phone. She just stood there smiling at me.

"Mom, you're creeping me out," I said. "Just give it to me. Please."

Mom handed me the phone and kept grinning.

"Privacy?" I said, frowning.

My mother raised her eyebrows.

I sighed and mouthed the words "I love you" while waving *buh-bye*. She left.

Okay. Yes. Boy on the phone. Do not panic. Please be Tristan, please be Tristan . . .

"Hello?" I said in a breezy American-girl voice.

"Uh, Claire? This is Callum."

Oh. Callum was cute and nice, too. Just not Tristan.

"Hey, Callum," I said cheerfully. After all, it wasn't *his* fault he wasn't Tristan.

"I, er, got your mother's phone number from the royal secretary," Callum said. "I hope that was all right."

"Sure," I said. "I should have given you my own cell number. Here it is." I gave him my number.

"Got it, thanks," he said. And then he hung up.

He hung up? That was it?

"Claire, a BOY called you." My mom's head popped through

my doorway. "And, you know how you promised that when you got your first love interest you'd share *everything* with me."

"Mom," I groaned. "I made that promise in like first grade!"

"And I've been waiting ever since," Mom said, and sat down on my bed.

I rolled my eyes. My mother and I had differing opinions on the appropriate age for boyfriends. I intended to focus on academics until I was at least sixteen. (Of course, it had helped that boys had focused on everything *but* me.)

"You're only young once," Mom said.

"You're right, Mum," I nodded thoughtfully. "I guess I'll come clean. I've found the chap I want to marry. We're in love, so we'll need to move to London straightaway so we can be together."

I clasped my hands in mock rapture. In response, I got a fluffy down pillow in the face.

"Luxury pillow fight!" I squealed and grabbed the nearest pillow and began whacking my mom. *Whump! Whump!* Soft down pillows did not make effective weapons. I dropped mine and went after my mother's weak spot. Her feet.

"Eeeeeeee!" she shrieked as I tickled them.

Mrrrow!

"What in the world is that?" Mom rolled away from me and sat up. I reached out and pulled my phone off the bedside table.

"Hello?" I said, keeping an eye on my mom, who was known for revenge tickle attacks.

"Hello, is this Claire?" a boy's voice said. I jumped up and looked at the caller's name. Tristan Symonds!

"Who is—," my mother started to say, but I waved her away with a "shh."

"Hi, Tristan." I looked at my mom and hit mute.

"I'm out the door," Mom said, smiling. "Find out his birthday so I can do your mutual astrology charts!"

Okay. Anyway. My mom left. I took a deep breath and unmuted.

"Claire," Tristan was saying, "Callum just rang me to give me your phone number. He had to call the prince directly to find out what hotel you were staying at. So that's how I found you. I hope that was all right. Not too stalkerish."

"Yrp," I said. "I mean YES. It's all right."

"Cool," Tristan said. "So. I was wondering. Tomorrow afternoon, my mum and Thalia are taking the Harry Potter walking tour. And me. I'm going, too. Would you like to join us?"

"Yes!" I said. "It sounds awesome." I started doing a silent happy dance around the room.

"Excellent," said Tristan. "Thalia's been wanting to go, and my mum said I should go too, to be nice to Thalia. Since she's not going to the wedding and all. Then I thought, well, maybe you'd consider going along, if you're not opposed to Harry Potter."

"I love Harry Potter," I said. (And even if I didn't, I'd go anyway! With Tristan!) *Woo-hoo!*

"Okay, we'll pick you up at your hotel at two o'clock," Tristan said.

"Jolly good," I responded.

"See you then," Tristan said, and hung up.

Jolly good? Where the heck did that come from? Medieval times? Couldn't I just be normal when talking to a cute boy?

Apparently not. I flung myself face down on my bed. "Mrrrow!" said my stomach. Oh. I was lying on my cell phone. I dug it out from under me and answered.

"Hello?"

"Claire-Bear, it's Belle," my cousin said.

"How are you?" I asked. *Considering people close to your fiancé's family are plotting to ruin your life, and I can't even talk with you about it?*

"I'm in a perpetual state of stress," Belle admitted. "Claire, did you know that they're predicting two billion people will be watching me get married? Two *billion*?"

"Whoa," I said. "Are you going to be able to do it?" *Am I going to be able to do it without going into full panic attack from stage fright? That is, of course, assuming the wedding will take place as planned . . .*

"Oh, I'll be able to do it," Belle said. "I'm just having prewedding jitters."

"Times two billion," I added.

"Well, on to the matter at hand," said Belle. "There has been a glitch in the assembling of the bridal party bouquets. So my maid of honor Justina must go to the florist first thing tomorrow morning to sort it out."

Belle paused. I waited, not sure where this was going. "So Justina will not make it in time," Belle said.

"In time for what?" I asked.

"In time for my final dress fitting," Belle said. "She was going to be brutally honest if there were things that didn't look quite right. So, Claire, will you come in her place? It will just be the designer and seamstress fussing over last-minute details, so it won't be very exciting."

"Are you kidding me?" I shrieked. "It's way exciting! I get to see The Dress? Everyone in the world would love to be there. Wow! Thank you so much, Belle!"

"Thank you for agreeing to keep me company," Belle said.

Then I remembered. Tomorrow was the Harry Potter tour. "What time is the fitting?" I asked.

"Seven o'clock a.m.," Belle replied. "My driver will pick you up at your hotel at 6:45."

Whew. It didn't interfere with my plans! I had *two* exciting things going on tomorrow.

"One more thing, Claire-Bear," my cousin said. "It's very important. Please tell nobody, except your mother. This is top secret. You know how the press would be if they even got a whiff of this."

"I promise," I said. "Cross my heart. My lips are sealed."

"It's such a relief to know that I can always count on you," my cousin said. "All those years when I visited, and we wrote all those letters to each other, and you never once told anyone our secret."

"I couldn't take a chance on losing you," I said.

I heard Belle sniffle. "Are you crying?" I asked. *Oh no. I made her cry. I'm not helping her.* "I didn't mean to upset you. Everything's going to be okay."

"I know," Belle sniffed again. "It's not you, Claire-Bear. I'm just a mess right now. Hold on, I need a tissue."

Oh boy. I knew what was coming next. *Wait for it . . . wait for it . . .*

"*HONK! Gah-Choo!*" Belle sneezed and blew her nose. *Honk! Aaaa-CHOO!*

I started giggling.

"Are you laughing at me?" Belle said.

"No, no, of course not," I said, giggling some more.

"Because if you are, I might not give you your special gift tomorrow," said Belle. "Laughing at the poor bride two days before her wedding. Imagine!" Belle was totally kidding, I could tell. But I stopped giggling anyway.

"I'm sorry," I said. "I'll be on my best behavior from now on."

"No, silly," my cousin said. "You just be yourself. I love

you, and I'll see you bright and early tomorrow morning."

We hung up. Be myself? Just a short time ago, "myself" was a shy nobody in a tiny tourist town. Now, I was going to be one of the very few people to see the princess's dress before the royal wedding, and I was going to a Harry Potter tour with a Cute Boy.

Eeeeeeeeeeeeeeeeeeeeeeeeeeeee!

I ran to tell my mother all the amazing plans, when a thought hit me. What if during the wedding vows, Belle got emotional? Two billion people would witness the honking-goose side of my cousin. I made a mental note to remind her not to sneeze or blow her nose during the ceremony.

Yikes. She'd told me to be myself, but for her that would be bad advice. In front of billions of people? With people trying to mess up the wedding? She was going to have to be PERFECT.

19

ROYAL WEDDING COUNTDOWN:
Only Two Days!

"It's perfect," I said.

"You're not just saying that?" Belle eyed me anxiously.

Belle was wearing The Dress, and The Designer was fussing over her. The überfamous designer whose fashions had been worn to the Oscars, the Emmys and other celebrity weddings. While her styles were classic and sophisticated, the designer herself was surprisingly frumpy in her jeans and tee and sneakers.

Her assistant, however, had an electric blue Mohawk, and he wore skinny black clothes and cowboy boots. As Belle discussed something with the intensely serious designer, the assistant winked at me. I smiled at him and then looked at Belle again.

"I mean it," I told her. "Absolute perfection."

I pulled a small notepad out of my pocket. I'd taken it from the hotel. I began writing a note with a pen that also had my hotel's name on it.

Dear Me,

I can't share this top secret moment with anyone but you (me). But I want to remember it forever. Belle is standing on a box in her wedding gown. From the neck up, she's regular Cousin Belle. Hair in loose ponytail, no makeup. And then you look down and WHOA. Her dress has this scoopy neckline that's not *too* low, and fitted long sleeves. It is made of white satin with *real* tiny diamonds around her neck and wrists. It goes down straight to her waist (hmm, when did she get so thin?) and then poufs out over layers of lace petticoats. The whole skirt part is white satin, and it has a long train in the back covered with beads and tiny sparkly diamond chips! It's elegant but not boring, and it makes her look incredible. OMG Belle picked the BEST WEDDING DRESS EVER!!!!!

"Claire," Belle said, standing straight and tall while the designer's assistant pinned her gown in a couple of places. "Tell me about how things have been going with you. Take my mind off this whole craziness for a bit."

"Everything has been amazing," I told her. "Better than I could have imagined. Did you know I get fresh flowers and a little chocolate on my pillow in my hotel room? I feel so pampered!"

Belle smiled.

"Well," she said. "You'll have a little more pampering tonight. Justina and my mom are throwing me a bachelorette party this evening. So my mother thought that you and your mum—and some of the others who aren't quite the "night out on the town" sort—would enjoy an evening at the spa."

"Really?" my voice squeaked. "I've never been to a spa. This is so cool!"

"I'll tell my mother you'd love to go," said Belle. "She's contacting your mom about the specific details."

"Oh," I remembered. "What time is the spa appointment? Because I kind of made plans for this afternoon."

Belle turned toward me, careful to move only her head

and not the whole dress. "Are these *fun* plans?" She raised an eyebrow.

"Yeah," I said casually. "I'm taking the Harry Potter tour with Thalia and Tristan and their mother."

"Sounds delightful." My cousin smiled. "The spa shouldn't interfere."

"Good!" I tried not to sound too relieved. I didn't want Belle to know I had a crush on Tristan. First, I was afraid she'd think it was silly. I mean, I'd just barely met him, and we lived on two totally different continents anyway. Second, this dress fitting was supposed to be about *her*—not me. Her dress. Her shoes . . .

"Belle," I said, "Are you wearing your shoes right now?"

"Oh." My cousin looked down. "You can't see them from under this big pouf, can you?" She lifted her dress enough to stick out her foot. She had on a white satin low-heeled pump. She wiggled it around a bit.

"Like it?" she asked. "It's got arch support and an anti-microbial lining to absorb perspiration."

"Ah!" I nodded. "The traditional princess shoe."

We burst into giggles.

"Careful," I said. "You don't want it to loosen up and fall off. You're Belle, not Cinderella."

"You said it, Cousin Claire." The designer's assistant suddenly spoke up for the first time.

"This girl?" he said, pointing a finger at my cousin. "She's no Disney cartoon. She doesn't need any Prince Charming to save *her* from a life of misery. She's a true princess with or without a man. Am I right or am I right, Cousin Claire?"

"You are right." I agreed with the designer's assistant. I was starting to like this guy.

"Yes, but without the man, you wouldn't be here doing your job," the designer muttered. "So how about getting back to work."

"I'm just saying," the assistant continued, kneeling down to fuss with a hem. "Fairy tales are just an illusion, blinding us to the reality of our fabulous selves."

We were all quiet for a moment. Did I even have a fabulous self? I wish I had more of the assistant's attitude.

"In reality," the designer smiled, "even this dress has some illusions. See, this is called an illusion neckline." The designer gestured at Belle's neckline.

"Oh, I get it," I said. "From far away, it looks like a scoop of white satin, but there's really also this . . . mesh . . . covering her up to her neck."

"Exactly," the designer said. "The flesh-colored hand-woven fabric allows her to display her décolletage while retaining the modesty befitting a princess."

"Uh—okay," I said. She'd lost me.

Belle smiled.

"There's another illusion on my dress," my cousin said. "See those tiny diamonds along my train, mixed in with the beads?"

I nodded.

"They're not real," Belle told me. "Fakes. Another illusion."

"They're not real?" I bent closer to take a look. "I can't tell. But what about the fashion police? The media? What if they notice they're not real diamonds?"

"Well, then *they* will get a lecture from me about the treatment of the people who work in the diamond mines. It will be a good opportunity to help expose the sad things that they're doing over there."

At that moment, I felt so proud of my cousin. She wasn't

being a spoiled diva or a Bridezilla. She was being her wonderful, caring self.

"You're so awesome," I said. "I'm so lucky you're my cousin."

"You're pretty great yourself," Belle said. "I can't imagine what I would have been like if I hadn't had those getaway vacation moments with you. They were so much fun, weren't they, Claire-Bear?"

"Yrp," I said, choking up.

"Ooh . . . we're having a moment," the designer's assistant sniffed. "Tissues! Tissues for everyone! No crying on the gown!" He tossed tissues into our hands.

The designer waved away the tissues and stepped back. She looked up and down at Belle. Then she circled around her.

"We're done," she said.

"Thank you so much!" Belle exclaimed. "You've done unbelievably wonderful work!"

"I shall see you at your preceremony room then," the designer nodded professionally. "My staff will be in shortly to help you undress. Do not move until they get here."

"I won't," Belle promised. The designer and her assistant

walked out of the room and shut the door. Silence. Then . . .

"Genius!" We heard the designer's happy voice out in the hall. "I'm a genius. Tell me I'm right. The whole world will fall in love with her in my dress."

Belle and I looked at each other, as we heard just a few words of her assistant's response as they went farther away.

"You're right! *Something something* champagne! *Something* . . . Cheers!"

Belle and I laughed.

"I chose that designer for her style," Belle giggled. "The hilarious interactions between her and her assistant are a bonus."

"They were funny," I agreed, happy to see my cousin so relaxed. And beautiful.

"All right," Belle said, turning serious. "It's a good time to give you your special gift." She gestured to a little table. "It's in that box. Would you please get it, seeing as I cannot move?"

"Of course," I said, running to the box. A present! It was a long, rectangular dark green box with a gold crown on it. I opened it.

"It's so pretty!" I sighed, pulling out a gold chain-link charm bracelet.

"Look at the charms," Belle urged. I carefully held it up toward the light.

"A cat who looks like the Beast!" I smiled. "An ice cream cone, a Scrabble tile—oh, 'cause I beat you in Scrabble that one time by like 200 points! A bear, for Claire-Bear . . . and a bell!" The bell was engraved with "Love, Belle" in teeny letters. "This is so amazing!" I slipped it on my wrist to admire.

"There's one more," Belle said, holding out her hand toward me. In her palm was a small gold crown. "When I say my vows, I'll become a member of the royal family. And that means, Claire, you will too."

Me? Part of the royal family? *Seriously?*

Before I could respond to, or really even process, what she'd just said, the door opened. A bunch of people rushed in and surrounded Belle.

"Claire-Bear! Have fun at the spa!" I heard Belle's voice over the others, who were muttering things like "Gently!" "Up!" "Over!" and "Don't faff about!" (whatever that meant).

"Okay, 'bye!" I shouted.

"And good luck with the boy wizard!" Belle called. "And I don't mean Harry! I mean the one who's cast a LOVE spell over you . . ."

I paused. *Aack. She meant Tristan. Em-bar-rass-ing!* I couldn't get *anything* past her. She knew me too well.

"Sorry!" I hollered. "Couldn't hear you!"

I slipped out of the room and headed down the hallway toward the exit. As I walked, the charms on my bracelet jingled softly.

Could any other eleven-year-old be so lucky?

Evie,

I feel like I've been transported to another world, an alternate universe where cute boys talk to me, and where magic can happen.

More later.

xoxo

Claire

P.S. I'll bring home some butterbeans for you.

"I will just die!" Thalia moaned dramatically. "I'm serious. I mean it!"

"Just put the hat on," Tristan said. Thalia shut her eyes and placed the sorting hat on her head.

"Gryffindor," an electronic voice announced.

"Yes!" Thalia punched the air. "Yes! Yes! I knew it!" Smiling, she took off the hat and gave it to me.

"Good luck, Claire," she said, as I put the hat on.

"Hufflepuff," said the hat.

"Awww . . ." Thalia looked disappointed. "Well, that's not so bad, Claire. It could be worse."

Thalia took the hat from me and plopped it on her mother's head.

"Slytherin," said the hat.

"Now *that's* worse," Thalia observed.

"I always knew I had a wicked streak in me." Lady Symonds winked and grinned at us. Next it was Tristan's turn.

"Hufflepuff."

"It looks like we're on the same team," Tristan said to me. *Yes! Yes, we are!*

"In the same *house*," Thalia corrected him. "This isn't football."

"Enough, kids," their mom said. "We're here to show Claire

a good time, not demonstrate the art of sibling bickering."

Lady Symonds seemed really nice. When I'd first been picked up at the hotel and saw her at the wheel of a shiny Range Rover, I'd been a little intimidated. She looked like one of the rich housewives on a TV reality series. But she'd been welcoming and funny, and even though Tristan (!!!) was so close (!!!), his mom managed to make me feel comfortable almost right away.

"Where do we go next?" Thalia asked the tour guide, an older gentleman who called us "Muggles."

"Wands," he said. He and Thalia walked off together, discussing the different varieties of wands.

"Oh, dear," Lady Symonds said. "I'd better keep an eye on Thalia so that she doesn't make too much of a pest of herself." She hurried to catch up with them. That left Tristan and me walking side by side.

"I'm really glad you invited me," I worked up the courage to say.

"I'm really glad that you're really glad," Tristan said. I glanced at him. He was smiling at me.

Okay. Cute boy with British accent smiling at me.

He was wearing a blue t-shirt, jeans, and skateboard shoes. And he was smiling at me.

Snap out of it, Claire.

"So, here we are," Tristan said. "Wands."

"Yep," I said. "Magic wands."

And that was the last brilliant thing I got to say to Tristan for a while. Thalia and the tour guide were trying to one-up each other with their encyclopedic knowledge of all things Potter, and Tristan's mother was asking me all about home and what it was like to keep such a big secret for so long.

Finally the tour ended. I was carrying a new wand, a bag of souvenirs, and a big box of butterbeans.

"Good-bye, Professor!" Thalia said to our guide, as he left us at the exit. "I'll e-mail you tonight with more trivia!"

"That poor man," Lady Symonds said.

"He said I was the most knowledgeable Rowling reader he'd ever met," Thalia said happily. She had a lightning bolt temporarily tattooed on her forehead.

A phone buzzed.

"That's for me," Lady Symonds said. "Why don't you all purchase some lunch at the café, while I take the call."

She gave Tristan some money. We went into the café, which served regular muggle food. It was rather crowded, but the line moved quickly and soon it was our turn. Tristan and Thalia ordered Marmite pitas and cherry fizzes. I was about to ask what marmite was, when I saw a cook spread grayish goops onto pita bread. I "ew"'d inwardly. And decided not to ask what marmite was.

"Um, do you have peanut butter sandwiches?" I asked.

"No peanut butter, miss," the man behind the counter said.

"Peanut butter isn't really an English thing," Thalia said. "They don't even sell it in the market."

I blushed. I hoped the people behind us didn't hear me. I was holding up the line.

"Don't worry about it," Tristan said to me. "You Americans are lucky. Peanut butter, burger drive-thrus, New York pizza . . ."

"Boys and food," I said. "I guess it's an international thing."

"Nachos . . ." Tristan droned on. "Or is that Mexico?"

"Okay, okay, you like food," Thalia said. "We get it. Claire, why don't you try bread and cheese?"

"Sounds good," I said. "That and a cherry fizz, please."

"Fab," Thalia said, and looked around. "While we wait for our orders, let's talk about Pandora and why she's acting like such a nutter."

"Thalia," Tristan groaned, looking around the crowded café. "Can't we do this another time?"

"There is no more time," Thalia protested. "The wedding is in two days."

"I agree that Pandora's been stirring up trouble, but is it really *that* important? It isn't like she can stop the wedding or anything," said Tristan.

"Well, Pandora can't," Thalia said. "But her great-aunt Cornelia can."

"What?!?" Both Tristan and I said at the same time.

"It's true!" Thalia said. "I . . . it's . . . she . . ." She tried to say something, but it wasn't coming out.

"Thalia, what's going on?" her brother asked.

But Thalia shook her head. She suddenly looked . . . scared.

"All right then." Tristan reached into his souvenir bag and pulled out his wand. *His wand?*

"This is the Wand of Truth," Tristan said. He pointed it at his sister. "It has the power to make you speak the truth."

Oh, no. Was Tristan starting to lose it? How did he think a fake plastic stick would make Thalia talk?

Tristan smacked Thalia lightly on her rear end.

"Hey!" Thalia jumped.

"Tell the truth, or the wand will get you again." Tristan began whacking Thalia—still rather gently—with his wand.

"Stop!" Thalia protested. Other customers looked over at us.

"I can't!" Tristan said. "It's not me! It's the Wand of Truth! It's out of control!"

"You are so weird, Tristan," Thalia said. "Okay, I'll tell you. Pandora's great-aunt is a witch."

"Surely you mean like a nasty person type of witch, don't you?" Tristan asked his sister.

"No," Thalia said quietly. There were a lot of people around us, but somehow all the noise seemed to fade into the background as Thalia finished her reply. "I mean a *witch* witch," she said.

Okay, I thought. *We already have a prince and a princess. Might as well add a witch to this tale.*

But then I looked at Thalia's pale face, her quivering lip. She was really scared. And as smart as she acted, she was only ten years old.

"It's okay, Thalia," Tristan said firmly. "Everything is going to be okay."

"Numbers twenty-four, twenty-five, and twenty-six!" a voice boomed over a loudspeaker. "Your order is ready. Twenty-four, twenty-five, twenty-six!"

"That's our food," Tristan said. "I'll go pick it up and bring it out to the car."

"Good idea," I said. "Come on, Thalia. Let's go out and find your mom."

Thalia nodded. We made our way through the crowd, and we were almost at the exit when Thalia grabbed my arm.

"I didn't tell you everything," she said. "I—"

"Claire! Thalia!" Lady Symonds called from the exit door-way. "It's beginning to rain!" She motioned us toward her. "Is Tristan coming?"

"Quick," Thalia said. "Give me your cell phone. I'll put my number in, and we can text during the drive."

"Good plan," I said. "We can get this all sorted out on the way back to the hotel."

I handed my phone over to her. We had a LOT to text about.

21

> ROYAL WEDDING COUNTDOWN:
> *Two Days*

Claire: It's me!

Thalia: Oh, good! Thx 4 giving me yr # to txt.

Claire: RU sure yr mom doesn't mind?

Thalia: She doesn't care unless Tris & I r fighting

Claire: Spking of Tristan, he wants to borrow this.

Thalia: Stop kicking the back of my seat—LTS

Claire: LTS? What does that mean?

(BTW, it's me, Claire again)

Thalia: My bro thinks he's funny. LTS = Lord Tristan Symonds. He calls himself that to bug me. Like I kick the back of his seat to bug him b/c I always get stuck in the way-back of the SUV when we have a guest.

Claire: Sorry

Thalia: No, not u! UR a gd guest.

Claire: The Big Q: Do u think Pandora is trying to sabotage my cousin?

Thalia: Yes.

Claire: Tristan wants to say something.

Claire: I agree w/my sister—LTS

Thalia: FOTF!

Claire: ???

Thalia: Fainting on the floor. FOTF. (b/c Tris agreed with me)

Claire: OK. So we all agree Pandora's up to no good.

Thalia: Yes. But I think Someone Else might be behind Pandora's weirdness. I call her She-Who-Must-Not-Be-Named.

Claire: You mean Great-Aunt Cornelia?

Thalia: !!!You named her!!!

Claire: How do u know her?

Thalia: Had a frightening encounter with her awhile back. And also—

"Hey," Thalia said from the way back. "What just happened?"

"What's wrong, darling?" Lady Symonds's eyes appeared in the rearview mirror.

"Nothing, Mom!" Thalia called. "Just . . . erm . . . Tristan."

"Behave, you two," Lady Symonds warned. "Claire shouldn't have to cope with your sibling rivalry."

"Nice," Tristan turned and hissed at his sister. "Toss *me* under the bus. Sibling rivalry? I'm almost fourteen. Sheesh." He shook his head.

Okay. I admit it. I know I was supposed to be one hundred percent upset and worried, because our phones disconnected and Thalia needed to tell me more about Great-Aunt Cornelia. And with Belle's wedding—really, her whole future—at risk, I had no time to be thinking about myself.

But . . . Tristan sitting in the seat next to me! Touching hands when we buckled our belts! Leaning into me when we took a sharp corner! Cutest boy closest to me in my (admittedly lame) history of proximity to boys.

And he didn't look unhappy about it.

Well, it was mildly distracting, to say the least.

Oof! I felt my seat bump forward.

I turned and whispered through the space between the seat and door. "Thalia, you kicked the wrong seat."

"Sorry," she whispered back. "I'm trying to get my cell to work and wasn't paying attention."

Tristan looked at me and . . . smiled. *Eeeee!*

"Hey, back there," Lady Symonds said. "You're making me a wee bit paranoid with all the whispering. I don't mean to pry, but are you sure everything is tip-top?"

"Yes," I said. "Tip-top. We were just trading stories about Belle and the prince. Like, um . . ." I thought fast. "Have I told you all about the time Belle came to visit me, and we were on a boat tour on the lake, and Belle almost got recognized?"

"No," Tristan said.

"Tell us," Lady Symonds said. "Tell us!"

So I launched into this (true!) story about how two British tourists insisted that Belle was the prince's girlfriend—even with her dyed-pink ponytails and fake tattoos. But then Belle started talking with this hilarious Southern accent and by the time we were saying "Bye, y'all" they were convinced they'd made a mistake.

Meanwhile, Thalia and I were tapping on our phones, trying to get them to work. No signal.

"Well, it sounds as if you and your cousin have had some lovely adventures," Lady Symonds said. She pulled the SUV over to a curb. "It was so nice of you to join us."

We were at my hotel! *Already? N-o-o-o!*

"Thank you for everything," I said to Tristan's mother,

while shooting Tristan a panicked glance to let him know Thalia and I hadn't finished our conversation.

Tristan leaned over. He started unbuckling my seat belt. "Allow me to help," he said. Then he whispered, "Keep your phone handy. We'll get ahold of you somehow."

"Yes," I said. "These seat belts are different over here." I smiled to show him I got the message. And because he was so cute and so close to me.

Thalia appeared over the backseat. "Bye, Claire," she said. "It was great meeting you." She looked sad.

Then it hit me. Thalia wasn't in the wedding party. I might not see her again!

"We'll talk soon," I promised. "Video chat. Maybe you could visit sometime."

"Oh, could we travel to the States, Mummy?" Thalia's mood brightened.

"That's certainly a possibility," Lady Symonds said. "But first, Claire has a wedding to prepare for."

She had no idea how unprepared I was. I got out of the car and ran through the rain, too quickly for the doorman to cover me with his umbrella.

I caught the reflection of the Range Rover driving away in the hotel's glass front. *Good-bye, Tristan.*

Sigh.

Now I had no choice. I had to be one hundred percent focused on Belle and her wedding. And getting my phone to work and discussing the whole Pandora–Great-Aunt Cornelia situation, whatever it was exactly, with Thalia.

I got into the elevator and waited. It didn't move. *Hello? Must ascend now!* Why wasn't it working?

Oh. I forgot to press my floor number. There. Going up. As the elevator rose, so did my anxiety level.

A few moments later, I was swiping my entry card. And swiping. The door buzzed red, and the door handle wouldn't move.

What is the problem with everything? Why isn't anything working??? First my cell phone, then my . . . oh. My key card was facing the wrong way.

Green light! Go! I opened the door and stumbled into the suite.

"Mom!" I called. "Mom-mom-mom!"

"What?" My mom came out of her room, yawning and stretching. "What-what-what?"

"My phone died," I said. "Where's yours? I need to borrow it."

"It's around here somewhere," Mom said. "I think it needs charging."

"But I have to talk to . . . I need to figure out . . . aack!" I ran around the room in a frenzy. "I need to use a phone!"

"The phones aren't working anyway." My mother said.

I stopped running. "What do you mean they're not working?" I said.

"Connections are sketchy all over London," Mom told me. "I saw it on the Internet just before my phone crashed on me. Apparently, everyone's buzzing about the wedding, and technology just isn't keeping up."

"But . . . but . . ." I paused. What could I say? I need my phone to work, so I can help save the wedding that's causing my phone not to work?

Uh. Maybe not.

Mrrrow. Meeeowww! Yes! It was working again!

"What in the world—" My mother jumped up onto a couch. "What is it? Where is it? KILL IT!"

"It's my phone!" I shrieked, ecstatic to hear the sick kitty ringtone. I ran into my luxury bedroom and shut the door behind me.

"Hello? Thalia?" I squealed and flung myself backwards on the bed.

And then I was flying back up through the air like a projectile away from the bed that I'd forgotten was so bouncy. I lost my grip on the phone, and I watched as if in slow motion as it left my hand and sailed toward the door I'd just slammed shut.

22

ROYAL WEDDING COUNTDOWN:
Two Days

(Letter dated two weeks after the engagement)

Dear Claire,

One of the things I love most about you is your honesty. So I will answer the question you posed in your last correspondence as truthfully as I can.

You wrote, "Belle, how can you deal with the entire world watching you, talking about you? It's a zillion times worse than middle school, and that's bad enough. How can you stand it?"

Well, Claire-Bear, it is really hard. I admit I've had my moments of tears and self-pity, especially when it comes to all the people who don't want ME to marry THEIR prince. There are all the girls who grew up dreaming of becoming the princess, like the so-called 'Throne Rangers' who show up at the places the prince is going to be, all prettied up, hoping to catch his eye.

Then there are the online groups such as Brits Against Boring Belle and the Keep Royalty Pure network, who want to keep me, a commoner, from polluting the royal bloodline.

And then there are members of the royal family, who I suspect are nice only to my face.

How do I deal with it? By proving them wrong. By holding myself with dignity and by loving my man. And trying to remember what matters. And who matters.

It's difficult, but it's not impossible. It's not so easy to know who to trust anymore, but I know I can count on you. If you ever need me, Claire-Bear, I'll be there. Just as I know you'll be there for me.

XOXO

Belle

The door opened, and my mom stepped into my room.

"Ow," I whimpered, still dazed from my wipeout. Mom jumped back a little and looked down.

"No time for resting," she said. "We have an appointment for the hotel spa in exactly two minutes."

"I need my phone," I said, reaching for it. I hoped it still worked, after its crash.

"No, Claire," Mom said. She leaned down and scooped it off the floor before I could get to it. "The spa receptionist said no electronic devices allowed. So, no phones."

She put my phone—*my phone*—in her handbag.

"Mom, do I *have* to go?" I asked. "I've got something really important to do here."

"Yes, you have to," my mother said. "Number one, it's a special gift from Belle, so it would look very ungrateful of you to skip it. And number two, hopefully they can do something about that acne breakout on your chin."

What? My hands flew up to cover my face.

"Now, let's go," Mom said. "I am *not* going to be late for my facial. There will be photographers and TV cameras everywhere at the wedding, and I need to look my best. Did you know that the camera adds ten years to your face?"

"I think that's ten pounds to your body, Mom," I groaned, getting up from the floor.

"That too?" my mother gasped. "Then I'll need the firm-up seaweed body wrap, also! And, Claire-Bear, I suggest you get the calming chamomile masque and mango-mint massage. You seem a bit tense."

Grrrr . . . I gritted my teeth and followed my mom out of our suite and into the elevator.

"May I *please* have my phone?" I begged.

"No," Mom said.

"Just one quick call?" I asked.

Ding! The elevator doors opened, and a fruity-scented mist wafted in.

"Welcome to the Zone of Zen," a woman dressed all in white greeted us. "Enter our sanctuary and leave your worries behind."

Leave my worries behind? Ha! Ha and ha.

"Hello!" my mom said eagerly, pushing me out of the elevator, into the spa.

"Come this way," the woman in white said, beckoning us. *Sigh.* I had no choice. I followed her.

Soon after, I was stretched out in a reclining chair, dressed only in a plush white robe.

"Ooh, it tickles!" My mother's voice came from behind a screen that separated us. We were in the same room but still had our privacy.

Except I could hear her. And smell her.

"Claire, this seaweed feels divine!" Mom called to me.

"Yay," I said half-heartedly. It *smelled* like fish that was long past its expiration date.

My attendant, whose name tag said "Karma," leaned over

me and placed cold cucumber slices on my eyes.

"Now just relax and imagine yourself in a peaceful, happy place," Karma said.

A happy place? I thought immediately about the banks of Lake George back home. During off-season, no tourists. Just a pebbly beach overlooking a serene blue lake . . .

I am lying on my back on the beach. The sun is shining down on me, and butterflies and dragonflies flutter peacefully around me.

Suddenly, dark storm clouds appear in the sky. Out of a cloud a figure appears, riding on a broomstick. It zooms down and swoops right over me. It's Pandora's great-aunt Cornelia! She lands next to me. I try to get up, to run, but I am frozen. I can't move.

"You shouldn't have opened Pandora's box," she sneers. She holds a shoebox over me, like one I kept in my closet for my child-hood princess stuff. I read the words "Pandora's Box" scrawled on it in pink marker.

Great-Aunt Cornelia opens the box and takes out a doll—a Disney princess Belle doll!—and dangles it by its hair over me.

"Mary, Queen of Scots and Lady Jane Gray," she intones. "Curse the royal wedding day!"

*And the doll's body drops onto me, with the old woman still
holding its head, and I scream. . . .*

"No!" I sat up, my heart pounding wildly. And almost col-
lided with a sunlamp.

"Honey, you've had a nightmare," a soothing voice said.

I peeled the cucumber slices off my eyes and saw Karma.
"Sorry," I said sheepishly. Karma flicked off the lamp, moved
it out of the way and swiped my face with a cloth.

"Your facial is done," Karma whispered. "I'll take you to
the mani-pedi room."

I put my bare feet in a pair of paper slippers that were next
to the chair. I shuffled over toward my mom's area.

"Shh," Karma said. "She's sleeping."

I peeked around the curtain. My mother was snoring, encased in a foil body wrap. She looked—well—like a
mummy. I left her and went with Karma into the hallway.

"Getting ready for the royal wedding must be so exciting!"
Karma squealed.

"Yup," I said.

I was still a little spooked from my nightmare. It didn't take a
genius to interpret it. Mary Queen of Scots and Lady Jane Gray

were two of the royals who had been beheaded at the Tower of London. And I, of course, had been worrying about Belle and the people who didn't want *her* to become a royal.

I shuffled along in my paper slippers. Karma was turning a corner ahead of me.

Suddenly, a door opened right next to me, and a face looked out. Not just any face—a hideous, green, lumpy face straight out of my nightmares!

"Aaagh!" I shrieked, jumping back from the door. Karma turned around.

"I want this goop off my face!" Great-Aunt Cornelia said from behind the green mask. "I have somewhere I need to be right now!"

"I'll go get your facialist, ma'am," Karma said, and hurried off, leaving me in the hall. With She-Who-Must-Not—*oh, forget it.*

She is just an impatient old lady, I told myself. *Woman up.* Maybe—hopefully—I was letting my imagination get away with me.

"What are you trying to do to my cousin?" I asked, trying not to let my voice quiver.

"Your cousin?" Great-Aunt Cornelia said. "So, you little American twit, you are not so dumb as my niece said you were."

"You *are* up to something," I said, not backing down. "I'm going to tell Belle, and she'll take care of you. And Pandora."

Great-Aunt Cornelia laughed.

"You think anyone would believe you?" she said. "You're just a nobody, while *I* am practically a member of the family."

I wanted to say, *Well, I WILL be a member of the royal family for real, and you can't stop that.*

But just then, a woman in white came running up the corridor with . . . my mom! In a white bathrobe, looking alarmed.

"Just give up now," the old lady hissed. "You cannot stop destiny!" She disappeared back into her room, shutting the door.

"Claire!" Mom said. "I forgot to turn off your phone!" She held out my phone (*my phone!*) as she reached me.

"We're suspending our no-call policy," the woman with my mother said, her eyes wide. "It's . . . it's the prince!"

"The prince?" I said. "Why is he calling *me?*"

My mother got very close to me and said softly into my ear, "Shh . . . Don't make a scene. Belle has called off the wedding!"

23

ROYAL WEDDING COUNTDOWN:
Two Days [*Maybe*]

Thalia: Claire!!!

Claire: UR back on!

Thalia: Mum and Dad took us out to dinner. No phones. UGH.

Claire: Update—the prince called me! Said Belle's upset over something & sez she can't marry him!

Thalia: What?

Claire: That's all I know. Mum & I are en route to the Palace.

Thalia: Is it the Curse?

Claire: What curse?

```
Thalia: That's what I need to
tell u about! Cn u call me? 2 hard
2 xplain in a txt.
    Claire: OK. Bye
```

"Mom, I've got to call Thalia," I said, punching in her number.

"What do you think is going on?" Mom said. Her hair still had bits of seaweed in it. She looked really upset. The first thing she'd said in the spa wasn't "Oh no—what if the wedding is called off" or "But I haven't had my massage yet." It was "We have to get to Belle!"

I sometimes forgot that I wasn't the only one who loved Belle. Mom did too.

"I don't know, Mummy," I said. "Let's try to find out." We'd both thrown on our clothes at the spa in record time and run out to jump in the limo the prince had sent for us.

"Hello, Claire?" Thalia answered her phone.

"Yes, Thalia, talk to me fast. We're almost at the palace," I said. I could see it as our limo drove past the horse stables known as the Royal Mews.

"Okay, last winter Mum took me over to Pandora's house to drop off some boxes for charity—"

"Pandora's house?" I couldn't help interrupting. "Charity?"

"Yes, her mom is always collecting for the needy," Thalia said. "She's nice—not at all like her daughter. Anyway, Great-Aunt Cornelia was in for a visit. I'd only met her once before and was scared to death of her, so when I spotted her I got so nervous I dropped the box I was carrying."

"And . . . ?" I prompted. We were idling in traffic, very close to the palace.

"And the toys slipped out, and this remote lorry—I mean, truck—started up and drove right at her, making her drop her teacup and spill tea all over her white suit," Thalia said. "So I was all like, 'Sorry' and 'It was an accident,' but she pointed her finger at me and said . . . she said . . ."

"She said *what*?" I urged, as the limo began moving forward again.

"She said, 'I curse you! You will suffer from the dreaded dropsy for the rest of your life!'" Thalia finished.

"Er—what's dropsy?" I asked. It sounded like a joke, but Thalia did not sound like she was kidding.

"A dropping things disease?" Thalia shrieked. "I guess. 'Cause ever since, I've been so clumsy dropping stuff. Oh! But that's not it. While Mum was with Pandora's mum, I saw Great-Aunt Cornelia spraying something all over Pandora and saying something in Latin, like Harry Potterish."

"Thalia, I saw Great-Aunt Cornelia spraying Pandora with something too! Do you know what it was?"

"No, but it gets worse," Thalia said. "At school the next day, I cornered Pandora in the halls and asked what that was all about. She looked at me and said, 'Oh, Auntie Cornelia? She's a witch. All those royal mishaps and tragedies? They were people who angered my auntie or got in her way.' And then . . ." Thalia stopped.

"Then what?" I prompted.

"Then," Thalia repeated, her voice small and scared, "Pandora threatened that her great-aunt would put a horrid curse on me and my family if I ever told anyone about this."

Yikes! I didn't say anything for a moment.

"Claire?" Thalia said, "You don't think I'm a nutter, do you? Because it sounds ridiculous, but it really seems like it could be true."

"Great-Aunt Cornelia is a real witch?" I said. "Thalia, I don't think you're crazy. Unfortunately, I think you might be right."

The limo pulled up at the main entrance, and security guards came to open our doors and hustle us inside. I hit the off button, shoved the phone into my jacket pocket, and ran to find my cousin.

"Good luck, honey!" My mother yelled.

I turned back to where my mom stood in the rain. "Aren't you coming?" I shouted.

"No, Belle needs *you!*" Mom responded. And as I headed back toward the entry door, I heard my mother yell, "Besides, I'm terrified of witches!"

24

<blockquote>
ROYAL WEDDING COUNTDOWN:
Cancelled???
</blockquote>

Belle,

I've knocked and knocked. This is the only way I can figure out to ask you to please please please let me in. I've met Justina, and she's told me what happened. I won't try to change your mind. I'm just worried.

Love,

Claire-Bear

I slid the paper under the door and crossed my fingers. Seconds went by . . . then a minute. I looked at Justina,

Belle's maid of honor, and shrugged sadly. "I tried," I whispered.

Then we heard the sound of the door unlocking. It opened a crack. "Come on in, Claire," Belle said. "And Justina, you too." Justina and I rushed in and shut the door behind us.

"Wow," Justina said, "This is the most fantastic loo I've ever seen! Thank you ever so much for inviting us in. Although, you do realize, as guest of honor at the bridal shower taking place outside, it would be proper for you to actually be there instead of here."

Belle was seated on the floor next to a very fancy toilet. She looked up and gave a weary half-smile. She was wearing a fancy black dress and black strappy heels.

As Justina tried to lighten the mood, I just stood there, feeling stupid. I had never seen my cousin look so . . . defeated. She'd obviously been crying. What was I thinking? I was just a kid from a small town in the States. How was I supposed to know what a princess in crisis needed?

Then, I realized, I didn't need to know that. I knew Belle.

"Sandwiches," I said to Justina. "Belle needs sandwiches. Preferably peanut butter and jelly. And chocolate milk."

Justina looked at me funny. But then she nodded.

"That sounds lovely," she said, as if I'd just requested caviar and champagne. "I'll go ring the kitchen."

"Thank you," I said, grateful that Justina seemed to understand that I needed some time alone with Belle.

Justina blew Belle a kiss and slipped quietly out the door.

I went over to Belle—it was a very large bathroom—and sat down on the floor next to her. I didn't say anything. She didn't say anything. We just sat.

I thought about the second summer that Belle visited. We were planning on going to the county fair, but it rained and rained that day. I was so disappointed. My mom made us PB and J sandwiches and chocolate milk, and we stayed in our pajamas and watched movies and played board games and talked.

It had been a wonderful day after all.

Knock. Knock. "It's me, Justina," a voice said through the door.

I got up and opened the door. Justina stood there, holding a tray of sandwiches and glasses of milk. She was tall, with catlike green eyes and black spirally hair. She looked at me for clues but I just shrugged. Nothing new to report.

"Belle," Justina said, "everyone is still out under the canopy in the courtyard. I told them to stay and enjoy the cocktails and food. I hope that's all right. Of course, everyone asked about you, and I told them not to worry. Belle, everyone who loves you supports you—no matter what you decide. We all just want you to be happy."

Belle sighed. "I know," she said. Her voice was a bit hoarse from crying. "It just all became too much."

"Well, of course," Justina said. "How are you supposed to feel when you're celebrating with your closest friends at your own bridal shower . . . and then your fiancé's ex-girlfriend walks into the party?"

"That's what happened?" I was shocked. Everyone knew about that über-blonde Swedish girl the prince had dated while he and Belle were on a 'break' from each other. It was in all the papers at that time, and the Swedish girl made sure to get plenty of publicity. I'd never met her, of course, but what I'd heard about her wasn't very nice. That was a bad, bad time for my cousin.

Fortunately, the prince and Belle had gotten back together

soon after. The prince had told the press that he'd made mistakes because of his immaturity, and he'd vowed to make it up to Belle.

And the Swedish girl hadn't been seen or heard from again . . . until now.

"How on earth did she get in?" Justina frowned. "It was a private party. And she looked so smug, I just wanted to smack her."

"Jussy," Belle said. "Relax, it wasn't just her. It's everything. I thought I could handle the stress, the scrutiny, the rules. But it's all too much. It's better to accept that now, rather than go through with the wedding and have our marriage fall apart later."

I wanted to cry. Belle sounded so tired, so un-Belle-like. And she looked way too thin.

"Um, let's move into the sitting room and have our snack," I suggested. The bathroom—no matter how fancy—was probably not the most hygienic place to eat. To my relief, Belle got up.

We sat on antique chairs with bone china plates in our laps. A small table in the middle held crystal goblets filled with chocolate milk.

"We don't picnic like this in Lake George," I muttered, taking a bite of sandwich. "What is this?" I said. "This isn't PB and J!"

"It's nutella with boysenberry jam," Justina said, calmly chewing. "The kitchen didn't have peanut butter."

"That's a chocolate and hazelnut spread," Belle told me.

"No peanut butter, no grape jelly," I grumbled. "This just isn't normal. No wonder you don't want to live like this."

I looked at Belle. She looked at her sandwich, then at me.

And we started cracking up.

"What?" Justina said. "What's so funny?"

"She's dumping the prince to live a normal life," I giggled. "With regular peanut butter and jelly and smushy white bread on paper plates."

"And plastic cups," Belle added, laughing harder. "Who drinks chocolate milk out of nineteenth-century crystal?"

Then I recalled what we had used on our indoor picnic back home. "And where are the paper napkins with mooses on them?" I demanded. "I want mooses!"

That put Belle over the edge. She dissolved into the hearty, snorty laughter I remembered from our summers together.

The laugh that was so contagious that soon Justina and I were laughing just as hard.

Suddenly, Belle got serious. *Uh-oh.* Was she going to cry again?

"It's 'moose,'" Belle said, all prim and proper. "Not 'mooses.' The plural of 'moose' is 'moose.' Now I'm going to finish my sandwich and then decide what to do with my life."

All three of us ate our sandwiches and drank milk until a young man in uniform appeared.

"Miss Belle!" he said. "Please, come quickly! It's urgent!"

Belle jumped up immediately. "I hope everyone is all right," she said. We all put down our food and drinks and followed the young man out of the sitting room, through another room, and then through a door.

We were outside, in a grassy courtyard. With about ten other people in cocktail dresses. I recognized Mags-Bags.

"Belle's friends," Justina whispered to me. "And *her.* The blonde party crasher."

I looked anxiously at my cousin. But she was staring into the small crowd, which parted in two, as if by plan.

So we had a better view of . . . the prince! On a stunning white horse, with a riding blanket showing the royal crest. He wore a red soldier's uniform and sat straight and tall and regal.

Suddenly, he dismounted, and still holding the reins he dropped down on one knee.

And started singing. Loudly. And quite badly.

"You are my dancing queen . . ." he crooned.

It's ABBA, I realized. Belle had played the seventies Swedish pop group's CD incessantly in Lake George.

Then, from behind the horse came Paul, the prince's best man, playing an accordion, also badly.

The prince stopped singing and spoke, holding his hand over his heart. "Belle, this is an original song I wrote for you."

He began to sing an over-the-top, cheese-filled love song with backup accordion. It was awful and wonderful and *romantic.*

"Belle, you're so swell, you're my dancing queen, and my one true love . . ." As the prince sang, the lyrics only got worse but the meaning was clear. The prince loved Belle with all his heart.

Awww . . .

When he was done, the prince looked at Belle. Everyone hushed. "Belle," the prince said, "I am making a fool of myself in front of all these lovely people to show how mad I am for you.

Crazy for you. And only you. The real you. And I can only hope that you'll accept the real, foolish, humble me as your husband."

"Truly?" Belle said. "Do you truly think I can do . . . all this? The media? The pressure? The wedding?

"WE can do all this," the prince said firmly. "Together. You're already strong. Together we will be that much stronger. Please, darling, will you marry me?"

My cousin thought for a long moment.

"Yes," she said, her face breaking into a happy smile. "Yes, I'll marry you. How about tomorrow?"

"Hurrah!" Everyone cheered and clapped and even the horse whinnied, which made everyone laugh.

Except, I noticed, the "blonde ex," who stomped away from the group. As she passed me to get to the door back into the palace, I heard her muttering highly unladylike words under her breath.

"The wedding is on!" The prince raised his fist in the air. He and Belle were beaming.

Yes! I was so happy, so relieved. The prince was obviously THE ONE for Belle. They deserved to be together forever.

Royal wedding countdown: Back ON!

Claire: Hi, Thalia! Great news! The wedding is back ON!

Thalia: YAY!!!!!!!!!!!!!!!!!!!!

Claire: I'll give u details another time. Mom & I are on our way back to the hotel for bed.

Thalia: Get yr beauty sleep. U hv a big morning 2morrow!

Claire: I know. I can't believe I'll be inside Westminster Abbey for the dress rehearsal. Wish u could be there.

Thalia: Me 2

Claire: 1 last question. How can
I find out who created the guest
list for Belle's bridal shower? I
don't have Justina's #.

Thalia: Let me ask Callum. He's
right here.

Claire: At your house?

Thalia: No. Didn't we tell you?
Tris & Mum & I have been staying
at Callum's father's townhouse in
Kensington. Wait. Callum sez he'll
call u. K?

Claire: OK

"Claire, you wanted to know about the guest invites to Belle's gathering last night?" Callum asked, after I'd answered my phone.

"If it's possible," I said. I looked over at my mother, who had mini headphones in her ears and was listening to music on her iPod. She had her eyes closed and was humming away.

Good. Although she was sitting by my side in the limo, my mom wasn't paying any attention to my conversation.

"It's possible," Callum said. "I'll just pull up my folder of guest databases on my laptop." I heard quiet tapping of keys.

"Don't do anything you're not supposed to," I told him.

"Oh, I have access to all the planning materials in case they need me to fix something," Callum said casually. "It's my job. Yes. Here it is—dated three weeks ago and signed off by the maid of honor, Justina Nathan."

"Okay," I sighed. That hadn't revealed anything.

"I'm not finished," Callum said. "There's a late addition on page two. Miss Melissa Skye."

"That's the ex-girlfriend! She crashed the bridal shower!" I shrieked. Mom looked over at me and raised her eyebrows.

"Page two was authorized by none other than Cornelia Quint," Callum stated.

"Great-Aunt Cornelia," I groaned.

"Claire, it's Thalia, you're on speaker now." Thalia's voice sounded farther away.

"I'm here too," Tristan said.

"Well, the good thing is that the old woman's plan backfired,"

I said. "Belle and the prince seem better than ever."

"Let's hope there are no more schemes or unpleasant sur-prises," said Tristan. "But if there are, Claire, just know that we are with you one hundred percent."

"I second that," Callum said.

"I third it," Thalia said. "Although it really should be ladies first."

"Who's a lady? You're a pipsqueak," Tristan teased, and I heard some thumping noises.

"Must break up sibling battle," Callum said.

"You guys are the best! Thanks!" I yelled, so that all of them could hear me, and then hung up.

"Claire," Mom said, removing her headphones and open-ing her eyes. "Are you finished shouting?"

"Um, yeah," I told her.

"Good," My mother said. "Because we've just pulled up at the hotel, and I need my beauty sleep. We have a wakeup call at six a.m."

"R-i-i-ght," I said. The limo driver came around to open my door, and I jumped out with a "Thank you." I had gotten used to this limo lifestyle quite quickly.

"I'm going to call Evie from the lobby," I told my mom.

"The reception's better there. Evie should be home from school by now."

"You have your key card?" Mom asked, as we walked up the stairway to our hotel. I nodded. I let my mother go first into the revolving door, and then I got in, taking an extra time around. Just for fun.

After an excited talk with Evie, I collapsed (carefully) into my luxury bed and slept a luxurious sleep.

When I woke up, my first thought was, *It's one day till the Royal Wedding!* I got ready as quickly as I could.

"Come on, Mom!" I called, slipping my foot into my shoe. "The limo's waiting downstairs!"

I was practically jumping up and down, I was so excited. I checked myself one last time in the full-length mirror. Nothing in my teeth, no rogue pieces of hair sprouting out from under my pale lavender headband, and my rehearsal dress was GOR-geous. Violet and white and swingy, and quite flattering on my non-model-like proportions. (If I did say so myself.)

"M-o-m!" I yelled. "We're going to be late for the rehearsal!"

My mother stumbled out of her room, putting an earring in.

"Need coffee," she said. I looked at her closely.

"First you need the other earring," I said.

Mom stumbled back into her room, hopefully to get it—and not to go back to bed.

Yes, it was very early. But it was the morning of the rehearsal on the day before Belle's wedding! *Eeeeee!* I did a little happy dance. Which turned into an impatient stomp.

"Mom! I'm leaving!" I called, hoping that would hurry her up. I opened the door that led to the hallway and stepped out.

Whoa! I practically tripped over a silver platter that lay on the floor outside our room. *Ooh, room service!* I hoped there was a cup of coffee for my mom under the fancy lid. In a to-go cup. And toast or a scone for me. I leaned down and lifted the lid.

"Aaack!" I jumped back and dropped the lid, which landed upside down next to the platter with a *clanggg*.

On the plate? A lock of brown hair tied with a red ribbon. *Ew!* Whose hair was that? I looked again. It was the same color as my hair . . . and Belle's. *What the—?*

Mrrrow! Meeeowww!

I pulled my phone out of my little drawstring purse that

matched my dress. Who would be calling at this hour?

It was a text. From a number I did not recognize. It was only one word: "CURSED."

"Mommy?" I whimpered.

"What, Claire?" my mother said, coming out behind me. I couldn't speak. I pointed down at the platter of hair.

"How disgusting," Mom frowned. "You'd think a fancy hotel would clean up better. Just ignore it. I'll make a complaint call to the desk later."

"But, Mom." I wanted to talk—*really* talk—about this creepy new development.

"I've got to get some coffee," my mom muttered. I stared at her back as she strode away and got into an elevator. I raced to keep up and hopped in just as the door closed.

I looked down at my phone again. "CURSED"! It was still there. I remembered Thalia's and my conversation. I had to talk with her ASAP. I realized it was early, but maybe Thalia would be awake. I called her number. I texted her. Nothing.

Mom stumbled out of the elevator after we reached the lobby. She headed straight for the breakfast buffet.

I'll call Callum! I thought, scrolling down to find his number.

He would definitely be up and getting ready for the rehearsal.

But his phone went straight to voice mail.

"Callum!" I said. "It's Claire! Call me!"

"Got my caffeine fix," my mother said, coming over to me. "And a muffin for you. Let's go, our limo should be outside."

It was. We got into the backseat. I texted Tristan. No response.

Where was everyone??? I was starting to freak out. "CURSED"! The lock of hair! Someone was threatening me! And no one was calling me back!

I wished I could get Evie's help, but it was like one o'clock in the morning back home, and her phone wouldn't be on.

Mom forced me to eat the muffin—admittedly delicious—as I sat quietly. As quietly as my phone. *Somebody! Call me! Text me!*

"Claire," Mom said. "We're here. Time to turn your phone off. Are you nervous? Excited? Oh, Claire, this is such a big moment. I'm so happy to share this with you." She choked up.

"Oh, Mom," I patted her shoulder. Clearly all of the coffee was affecting her.

Please someone call me! I shrieked inside my head. I waited a few more seconds before reluctantly shutting my phone off.

The chauffeur helped me and Mom out in front of the church where the rehearsal was being held.

"Wow," Mom breathed.

"Double wow," I agreed.

It wasn't just any church. It was Westminster Abbey, the spectacular stone and stained glass cathedral that had been the site of over one thousand years of English history. Kings and queens had been crowned inside and also buried in tombs here. It was a place to celebrate life and to commemorate the dead.

Then I shuddered. It was at times like this I really wished I didn't know so much about Britain's history.

There were no tourists or crowds around the cathedral. Officers on horseback stood guard as far as the eye could see.

My legs felt shaky and my stomach was in knots, but I took a deep breath, pasted a smile on my face, and walked arm in arm with my mother into Westminster Abbey.

26

ROYAL WEDDING COUNTDOWN:
Twenty-four Hours

Response card mailed back to the Palace six weeks before:

MISS CLAIRE E. GROSS AND MS. DEBRA GROSS

☑ *Accept with pleasure*

☐ *Decline with regrets*

I stood in my proper place in line, along with the others in Belle's bridal party. Justina was closest to the altar. Next came the three senior bridesmaids. Then me! Pandora stood just behind me (so much for her being the *head* junior bridesmaid) and last were the two adorable flower girls.

I had waited patiently through all the wedding planners' instructions, stood quietly while the archbishop recited ceremonial words, and kept silent during the choir's practice.

But inside, I was jumpy and restless and anxious. When the wedding planner had been lining us up, Pan-*diva* took the opportunity to kick me in the ankle. Besides that, though, not one thing had happened to suggest that the wedding was in jeopardy or that tomorrow wouldn't go smoothly.

I wanted to confront Pandora about that text— "CURSED". Was it her? Could she have tampered with room service? Or did her great-aunt orchestrate the whole thing?

What was the curse? What did it all mean? What was I supposed to do??? I looked around the cathedral.

I had a partial view of Belle's and the prince's backs, as they stood up on the podium. Belle wore a simple navy sheath dress. The prince stood tall in a dark gray suit.

I couldn't see my mother, who was sitting somewhere with the hundred or so family members and close friends in the pews.

I sneaked a peak over at the line of guys standing up for the prince. I saw Callum, with his fluffy blonde hair slicked down with gel. And next to him was Tristan. Looking totally handsome in a navy suit with a red tie.

Okay. We'd been here for a while now. The tissue paper flower bouquet I'd been given to substitute for the real thing was beginning to droop in my tense grip. Maybe I'd been wrong. Maybe nothing was going to happen. Maybe Callum and his crew had figured out what to do. Maybe my cousin Belle would have her happily ever after, after all. I closed my eyes and took in a deep, cleansing breath.

And heard the archbishop say in his rich, booming voice, "If there is any known reason this man and this woman should not be joined in holy matrimony, please speak now or forever hold your . . ."

"STOP!"

My eyes flew open. Everyone gasped and turned to look in my direction.

Well, not exactly *mine*. Pandora's!

"Stop this madness now!" Pandora shrieked, throwing her paper bouquet on the floor and stomping on it.

Belle's gentle voice broke through the shocked silence.

"Pandora," she asked, "Why?"

"The love curse!" Pandora declared. "This marriage has been cursed, and it is doomed!"

I could *not* believe this was actually happening. Apparently, nobody else could either, because nobody moved. But then I noticed a figure wearing a large-brimmed black hat trying to make her way out of an aisle near the back.

"It's Great-Aunt Cornelia!" Tristan called out. "She's leaving!"

"Out of my way!" Great-Aunt Cornelia snapped at an usher who stood at the end of her row. Her voice echoed loudly through the hushed room.

"Cornelia!" a voice called out. And Great-Aunt Cornelia froze.

It was the queen!!!

The queen of England stood up in the front pew and turned around. She was wearing a teal dress and matching hat, with a peacock feather sticking out of it.

"Cornelia!" she repeated, her voice sounding as steely as her tight gray curls. "You are making a scene! Come up here and explain yourself!"

Oh. My. Gosh.

I didn't dare move out of my position, and I'd been sternly instructed by the wedding coordinator not to speak unless personally spoken to. Great-Aunt Cornelia shuffled her way to the front in her sensible black shoes. I looked at Belle and the prince, who were now standing close together near the archbishop. Justina, the maid of honor, had gone up to support Belle. I looked over at Tristan and Callum. They were whispering to each other.

I wished I had someone to whisper to. I was stuck next to . . .

"Pandora!" I whispered loudly. "Pssst . . . Pandora!"

She pretended not to hear me.

Great-Aunt Cornelia had made her way to the front pew. The queen said something to her that I couldn't hear, and then Great-Aunt Cornelia turned to face the audience.

"I suppose I must apologize for telling my grandniece that I had placed a curse on this lovely bride," Great-Aunt Cornelia said to everyone. "I was just having a little fun."

The queen glared at her and then spoke again.

"Cornelia," she said imperiously, "was jilted by my uncle, a prince, who chose to marry another woman many, many decades ago. Evidently, she has still not quite recovered from being excluded from our family. But really Corny, you have gone too far! A curse? What nonsense!"

"Wait one moment," one of the groomsmen, a tall man with a thin mustache, stepped forward. "Aunt Cornelia, when I was a young boy, you told me that if I didn't get into Eton, where my father had gone to school, I would suffer from the 'moron's curse' and never amount to anything in life. Was that not true?"

The old woman hung her head, her black hat hiding her face.

Then a small voice near me piped up. It was one of the flower girls!

"Auntie Corny?" she said. "Am I still cursed by the Green Knight, because I didn't eat my green vegetables?"

And then a few others joined the curse chorus, and it became clear that Great-Aunt Cornelia had been telling generations of upper-crust British children about curses for fun.

For fun?

"Excuse me!" I said, shakily. No one paid attention to me. I took a deep breath. "EXCUSE ME!"

Everyone stopped talking and looked at me. I kept my eyes on Belle, who was now nodding at me.

"Claire," my cousin said, "go ahead."

"I don't think that leaving a lock of hair with a threatening message is very funny," I said.

"What?" Great-Aunt Cornelia looked up. She looked truly confused. "I don't know anything about a lock of hair. As I told you, this is all just a little misunderstanding. I'd like to go back to my flat—"

"No!" Pandora screamed. "Auntie! What about the love curse? What about our family legacy? You can't let this wedding go on!"

"Oh, my dear girl," Great-Aunt Cornelia said. "I made that whole love curse thing up. You are the one who is sweet on the prince and want to marry him yourself!"

"*It was you*, Pandora!" I cried. "You've been trying to sabotage Belle all week long, and you left that freaky hair scare message!"

"Oh, Claire-Bear!" Belle said.

"Oh, Pandy-Bear!" A woman in the audience stood up.

"Quiet, mother," Pandora hissed. Then she turned to me. "You don't know anything! You have no proof!"

"Yes, she does!" Thalia burst in through the back door, along with Daphne and Gus—who were in police uniforms!

"We parked next to Pandora's family's car in the parking

lot, and I found *this* hanging out of the car door!" Thalia shouted. She held up a doll that looked like Belle—with most of its hair cut off!

Pandora looked around wildly.

"Aunt Corny?" she said. "What about the magic spray? To make my dreams come true?"

"Just water," Great-Aunt Cornelia admitted, as security guards took her arms and led her away.

I looked at Pandora, who suddenly seemed rather pitiful. "Pandora," I said, thinking that *maybe* she'd been just a victim in all this too, "it was all a mistake."

"There is no mistake." Pandora turned on me, her face red and her eyes blazing. "This is all your fault! My family's legacy is going to be restored! It's my destiny! I am the rightful princess, and this should be *my* wedding!"

I looked Pandora straight in the eye. "Pandora," I said loud and clear. "You have been cordially *UN*-invited!"

And Daphne and Gus rushed up and grabbed Pandora. As they dragged her away, she shrieked, "But we *cursed* them! *I'm* supposed to marry the prince! *Meeeee . . .*" And the heavy cathedral doors closed behind them.

The church was suddenly completely quiet.

Then Thalia shouted "Hurrah!" And Callum yelled, "Three cheers for the bride and groom!"

As the crowd yelled "Hurrah!" I glanced at Tristan. He was looking at me and smiling! He gave me a thumbs-up. I gave him a thumbs-up back. With a big smile.

We'd actually done it! Outwitted Pandora, exposed Great-Aunt Cornelia, and saved the wedding! I couldn't wait to tell Evie! I couldn't wait to celebrate with my new friends! I couldn't wait for Belle to become an official princess.

The cheers finally died down.

"Well," the queen announced regally, "with all that non-sense taken care of, let's proceed!"

So Belle and the prince turned back to face each other, and the archbishop began speaking, picking up where he'd left off.

I held my paper bouquet and stood between the senior bridesmaid and a Pandora-shaped gap. And I didn't stop smiling all the way through the rest of the rehearsal ceremony. Which went perfectly.

27

ROYAL WEDDING COUNTDOWN:
Minutes Away

EV—This is it! On way to The Wedding!
Nrvus but xcited! All quiet since
Curse Chaos & Pandora plan failed. My
dress & shoes r tres chic! Hair clip—
not so much. LOL We're here! Aaack!

"Claire," my mother said, "stop fussing with your hair."

"It's my hair clip," I said. "It won't stay in right."

Mom leaned over, unclipped me, smoothed my hair, and reclipped. "Your hair looks so sweet," my mom said.

"I don't want to look sweet!" I protested. "I'm a junior bridesmaid, not a flower girl!"

"You look beautiful and elegant, and I'm so proud of you," Mom sniffed. "Oh, don't let me cry my eyelashes off!"

The limo driver opened our door to let us out. I carefully swung myself around so that my blush pink dress with lace trim wouldn't get wrinkled or caught on anything. The driver helped me out, and when I stood, my dress swirled around my legs. I felt like a gauzy butterfly.

"We love Belle!" "We love the prince!" "For he's a jolly good fellow!"

I couldn't see anything over or between the security guards who escorted my mom and me into the abbey. But I could sure hear a lot. Besides people chanting and cheering, there were bells and trumpets. It sounded like a party out there. I was glad people were happy for Belle, for their prince, and for their country.

Mostly, I was glad to be a part of it.

Within fifteen minutes my mother had been whisked away and the wedding coordinator had guided me to my place in line. I turned and said hi to the adorable flower girls Lizzie and Lyla. Then I said a big, happy hello to the person who had taken Pandora's place.

It was Thalia!

"This is so surreal," Thalia said. "Claire, how can I ever thank you and Belle for this?"

"Oh, you deserved it!" I told her. "You helped a lot. Plus, you fit in the dress." We cracked up.

"It's the first time I've actually been grateful for being tall for my age." Thalia's brown eyes sparkled and the highlights in her red-gold hair shone under the lights.

I looked up. The stained glass windows and the arched ceiling were so high and spectacular. I looked across and saw Tristan and Callum in red, black, and gold jackets with turned-up collars. They looked handsome and serious.

I tried very hard not to think about the hundreds of glamorously attired guests or the thousands of well-wishers outside or the millions around the world who were watching on TV, over the Internet, on their computers. This was the world's wedding, but it was also a family celebration.

And then, it was time.

The organist began playing the traditional wedding march, and the entry doors opened.

The audience gasped. Framed in the doorway was the most famous bride on earth. She glided in on the arm of her father. The bride looked stunning, with her long, thick auburn hair done up in a loose bun, with small pieces curling out and framing her glowing face. Her bouquet of white irises and pale peach roses was in full bloom. And, of course: The Dress. The dress that everyone would be talking about for weeks afterward.

Wow, I thought. I sneaked a peek at the groom. He was wearing full military uniform, polished and handsome. He was grinning. The bride and her father were coming closer, making their way toward the altar. When they reached the front, the bride's father lifted her veil off her face and over her head and kissed her cheek. The bride leaned over to hand her bouquet to her best friend, the maid of honor.

And then the bride looked straight at me . . . and winked!

I gave her a little smile. I was standing perfectly still in the line of bridesmaids, but on the inside? Total jitters. If I hadn't been gripping my own bouquet so hard, I'd be biting my manicured nails. Thoughts were exploding in my head like fireworks. The evil plot! The love curse! Me—Claire Gross— in the royal wedding of the century! And not messing it up.

That's right. Even though during that palace dinner (was it only four days ago?) Pandora had tried to make me insecure about, well, everything, I was the one standing tall and proud. No tripping up the aisle! No accidentally dragging a piece of newspaper stuck to my heel (because I noticed it and peeled it off before even entering the church)!

And no full-blown hyperventilating panic attack where they had to carry me out on a stretcher, wheezing and moaning! (Which had happened in the worst wedding-related nightmare I'd had back in the States.)

The moment had come! Would it end up in disaster, with the "I dos" becoming "I don'ts"? Or would goodness prevail, with my lovely, funny cousin marrying her prince and having her dreams come true?

I focused back on the ceremony. The bride and groom were facing each other! It was almost time for the vows! A hush fell over the room.

That's when I opened my mouth. It couldn't be helped—I absolutely had to let it out.

I'm sorry, I thought, tears welling up in my eyes.

And then I did it.

I interrupted the royal wedding of the century.

"Ah-choo!"

I sneezed. Thankfully, it was a rather quiet, delicate sneeze. I held my flower bouquet a bit lower, in case it was the cause of my sneeze.

And then, along with the rest of the world, I watched my cousin get married.

ROYAL RECEPTION

Dear Belle,

Once upon a time, a handsome prince married a beautiful princess at a fairy tale wedding. And they lived happily—and realistically—ever after.

Love,

Claire

"May I have this dance?" Tristan asked me.

We were at the wedding reception, in a grand state room at Buck House (what the locals called the palace). There were white calla lilies, tall white candles in gleaming silver candlesticks. And many, many people.

At this moment, though, there was only one person I was smiling at.

"Definitely," I said, and Tristan and I went out to the dance floor. I put my hands around his neck, and he held on to my waist. I had taken a couple basic lessons back home before the wedding so that I wouldn't look too foolish dancing. Of course, back then I didn't imagine I'd be using those skills with a very cute British boy.

"Wild week, huh?" Tristan said. "With preparing for a wedding, hanging out with the royals, and foiling Pandora's preposterous plan!"

"And meeting you . . . and Thalia," I added, trying not to step on his feet. My low-heeled shoes added an inch to my height, so I could look into Tristan's eyes without tilting my head back. Which I did, meeting his gaze.

"For me, that was the best part," Tristan said. "I mean, meeting you—not Thalia." He blushed.

Awwwww . . .

"What *about* Thalia?" Tristan's sister asked suspiciously. She and her dance partner, a page boy who was about a half foot shorter than her, box-stepped their way over to us.

"Only good things," I assured her. The song came to an end, and I reluctantly took my hands off Tristan's neck and stepped back.

"They're cutting the cake in the picture gallery!" Lizzie the flower girl was running around, announcing it to everyone.

"Cake?" Tristan's eyebrows went up.

Thalia and I laughed. The three of us made our way into the picture gallery, where we watched Belle and the prince slice into an eight-layer cake of cream and white icing and sugar-paste flowers.

Soon after, we were happily eating cake at our table—Tristan, Thalia, Callum, and me. I was finishing up my last bite, when there was a tap on my shoulder.

I looked up at Belle. She had changed into a white strapless evening gown and held hands with her black-tuxedo-clad husband.

"Congratulations," I said, managing to swallow the cake first. Was I supposed to get up? Should I curtsy?

"Stay seated everyone," the prince said. He held up a fancy camera. "I borrowed this from the official photographer, at my *wife's* request."

"Wait, darling," Belle said. "First I need to give Claire-Bear her gift."

My gift? What else could possibly make me happier than I was right now?

Belle handed me . . . a Belle doll.

"Um, thank you?" I said. It took a couple of seconds, but then I saw it. The doll had short hair and was wearing a small black hat—embroidered with a pink skull.

"Mags-Bags!" I laughed. "Did she make this hat?"

"She transformed the 'curse' doll into a happy souvenir for you," Belle said, pointing out the doll's sash that said I ♥ CLAIRE and the teeny gold ring painted on its tiny finger.

"It's perfect!" I squealed, and held up the doll for everyone to see. Thalia clapped and Tristan and Callum laughed.

"Photo time!" the prince said. Belle leaned down so that her face was next to mine, and the Belle doll was in the picture, too.

The prince snapped it.

"I wish Evie could see this," I said.

"Darling," Belle said, "Take another one on your cell phone, please. We'll e-mail it to Evie and she can forward it to your friends back home."

"Really?" I gasped. No guests had been allowed to bring cell phones or other devices into the wedding or reception. Only official wedding photos would be released to the media.

"Really." Belle grinned, and I did too, this time holding the doll under the table. *Click!* The prince took the picture.

"Here you go," he said, giving me the phone. "Send it to whomever you'd like. Find me later to return it and have a dance with me, if you'd like."

Gulp.

That guy really was Prince Charming. And the perfect husband for Belle.

As the prince and Belle left to mingle with the rest of the guests, I felt something drop into my lap. It was an ivory-colored envelope with the name "Claire-Bear" written on it in fancy gold script.

I felt a lump in my throat. Belle would be leaving for her honeymoon, and for the rest of her life as a royal. I would go home, and we would go back to keeping in touch by letters in the mail, but now without the secret visits from my undercover "Australian" cousin. *Sigh.*

When would I see my cousin again?

I looked around the table at beaming Thalia, brilliant Callum—and Tristan, who was eating his second (!) piece of cake.

When would I see *them* again?

I felt like I might burst into tears. I quickly excused myself, holding tightly to the envelope, and got up from the table. I hurried off to the ladies' room. I was almost there, when I nearly bumped into someone.

"Pardon me," I said, and then stopped short. And dropped into a curtsy. "Your Majesty."

The queen looked at me. Then she nodded her head and her tight lips turned up into a small smile. "You look lovely," the queen said, "Cousin Claire."

As she and her entourage moved away, I stood there with my jaw practically to the floor.

The queen of England knew who I was!

I walked carefully onward.

Plantagenet, Lancaster, York, Tudor, Stuart, Hanover . . . Windsor! The House of Windsor—my new family. I shook my head in wonder.

I was ready to live happily (enough) ever after.

EV—Here's a photo taken with the prince's phone!

Claire!!! You and Belle look so happy! Awesome pic! I saw you on TV! Everybody did! The wedding looked amazing! But we all want to know—what was with the crazy hats??? You were lucky to just have that hair clip—LOL—EV

EV—ROTBFL. (Rolling on the bathroom floor laughing.) Yep. In the royal restroom. I shouldn't be using the

prince's phone, but let's just say
I have a HUGE, exciting surprise
for you!

I put the phone down on a counter and took an envelope
out of my little drawstring bag. I pulled the note from the
envelope and read it for the third time.

> Dear Claire-Bear,
> Thank you for everything! I hope you
> enjoyed your visit! I've enclosed a little
> something for you, your mum, and Evie—to
> be used during your summer holiday.
> XOXO
> Belle

Then I reached into the envelope and took out three
first-class round-trip airplane tickets from New York to
London.

I was cordially invited back to London! With Mom
and Evie! Second royal visit countdown—sixty-something
days!

I tucked the tickets and the note back into the envelope and dropped them in my bag. I looked in the mirror over the antique sink and applied some pink lipshine.

Then I opened the door and went out to rejoin the celebration.

– The End –